MISSPELLED

MISS PRIMM'S ACADEMY
FOR WAYWARD WITCHES: BOOK 1

CHRISTINE POPE

MISSPELLED

Copyright © 2021 by Christine Pope

ISBN: 978-1-946435-46-0

Published by Dark Valentine Press

Cover design by Christian Willmanns/Taurus Colosseum

Ebook formatting by Indie Author Services

CHAPTER 1

LEAVING HOME

I clicked the latch on my suitcase, holding my breath as I wondered whether the minor locking spell would actually work this time. Such a simple enchantment should have been as easy as breathing...but magic and I weren't precisely on speaking terms most days.

But the lock held, even as I thought how final a sound that soft little *snick* was. No matter what happened over the course of the next three years, the room where I stood—the room that had been mine ever since I was old enough to go toddling about the house on my own—would never be home to me again.

Either I would somehow manage to get my unruly magic to behave itself during my tenure at Miss Primm's Academy for Wayward Witches...or

I would be banished to Mundania just like all the other poor souls in the world whose magic had failed them.

A soft swish of fabric made me look up from the suitcase. My mother stood at the door to my bedroom, her forehead creased with the faintest of frowns. We resembled one another a good deal, with our bright blonde hair and clear blue eyes, although she exuded a serenity I doubted I would ever be able to achieve, even if I did somehow manage to get my magic under control. Her own particular gifts extended to everything domestic, up to and including the marvelously complicated hairstyle she wore, although, like most witches, she had mastered a wide variety of spells.

My own hair fell in waves nearly to my waist —pretty enough, I supposed, but I knew better than to attempt any sort of enchantment to coax it into braids and rolls like my mother's hair. The one time I'd tried to do something magical to my long locks, they'd seized up in frizzy corkscrews that had taken the better part of a week to comb out.

"It's going to be fine, Callie," my mother said. No doubt I'd been wearing a frown to match her own, although, since I wasn't standing in front of a mirror, I couldn't precisely see my own face to know for sure. "Why, you know your Great-

Grandmother Fern also attended Miss Primm's, and she turned out to be an exceedingly gifted witch."

This was a story I'd heard many times before, ever since it became painfully obvious to me and my entire family that the only way I could make something of myself—and not get banished to that terrible place where magic wasn't real, was only a fairy story told in uncounted books and films—was to go to Miss Primm's academy and hope that worthy institution could set me on a path to magical accomplishment. Any witch or wizard who could not satisfactorily complete their secondary assignments was given three more years to whip their magic into shape, either at Miss Primm's for us girls, or Master Marco's School for Woeful Wizards for young men.

But even though I knew my situation was unfortunate, it was not unprecedented. For the hundredth time, I reminded myself that these post-secondary schools would not exist at all if they weren't effective. True, they'd had their failures, but those unfortunate students who'd failed and therefore became lost to this world were definitely the minority. I had every reason to think I would be yet another of Miss Primm's success stories.

Well, that was what I told myself, anyway.

Unfortunately, my magic was so very unruly, I wondered if even the instructors at the academy could get it straightened out. A spell to protect my mother's vegetable garden had attracted every voracious insect within a five-mile radius. The enchantment I cast to make sure the cake I was baking for her forty-fifth birthday party wouldn't fall instead sent the thing flying around the kitchen like a maddened pancake until we were able to use a broom to knock the crazed confection out of the air. Even then, we had to beat on it for a least a minute before it subsided and returned to its constituent ingredients, leaving a mess of flour and milk and raw eggs on the kitchen floor.

Because of incidents like that, I honestly didn't know for sure whether or not I was at all salvageable. Still, I had to try.

"Oh, I know it will all turn out in the end," I said airily, doing my best to sound cheerful and not at all troubled by the prospect of spending the next three years far away from my family.

I couldn't say I'd miss my friends, because honestly, I didn't have any. No one at my school had wanted to associate with a walking disaster like Callie Dobkins, and so the only people in my immediate circle were my mother, my brother Jacob, and my two sisters, Holly and Rose. However, as both my sisters and my brother were several years older than I—and very accomplished magic practitioners in their own right—they had already moved out of the house and begun the adult portion of their lives. Why, Holly had just sent word the week before that she was engaged.

While I was happy for her, I couldn't help feeling just the slightest bit jealous. Not that I had any desire to be engaged at only eighteen, but still, she seemed to have everything going her way, whereas I....

Well, let's just say that no self-respecting wizard wanted to get too close to a witch who might make all his hair fall out or compel his nose to grow by six inches, simply because of a spell gone horribly wrong.

My mother smiled, the faint frown she'd worn a moment earlier gone as if it had never been there in the first place. It was her task to see me off to Miss Primm's, for my father was busy with his work at DOME—the Department of Magical Exile. The wizards and witches who worked there were the ones who oversaw the removal of those whose magic either never developed at all, or which couldn't be contained, like mine.

More than once, I'd thought of what an embarrassment I must be for him, for someone who worked at that particular agency to have a daughter who might have to suffer the same fate as the poor souls he and his colleagues sent off to

Mundania. If it should come to that for me, would he be the one tasked with that horrible assignment, or would one of his fellow agents take pity on him and handle the job in his stead?

I did my best to shove that awful mental image aside, and reminded myself I had three years to avoid such a terrible fate. Three entire years, to be completely accurate, because one of the requirements of attending Miss Primm's academy—or Master Marco's school—was that we spend the entire duration of our training there. No summer holidays, no break to come home for the traditional midwinter festivities. The logic behind these rules was that the schools wanted to make sure none of their pupils were exposed to outside influences while they were trying to bring their magic under control, but it still seemed very harsh to me. I had never spent even a weekend away from home, and now I would have to endure a whole three years without seeing my family.

But it was all for the best. This was my last chance, after all.

"Are you ready?" my mother asked then.

I nodded, and clicked my tongue against my teeth. At once, Flotsam and Jetsam, my two gerbil familiars, popped out from behind the bed and scampered over to me so they could jump onto my shoulders, their favorite perch.

Yes, I know. They perhaps weren't what I would have chosen for myself, if given the opportunity, but the familiar—or familiars—chose the witch, and not vice versa. Having such familiars was perhaps the earliest sign that my magic wouldn't live up to the Dobkins family's magical reputation, since everyone else had much more impressive companions. My mother's familiar was a sleek black cat, my father's a magnificent falcon. Holly had a beautiful albino python, while Rose was accompanied everywhere by a lovely robin, and Jacob's familiar was a clever little ferret.

But Flo and Sam, as I called them, were certainly affectionate and amusing to have around, even if they didn't do very much to assist me with my magic. Their sharp little claws gripped my red cardigan—part of the school uniform—as I picked up my suitcase and met my mother out in the hallway. Bright sunlight streamed through the diamond-paned windows, and as always, the air had just the faintest fragrance of honey from the beeswax my mother's enchantments employed to condition the woodwork and keep it shiny.

The house had been in the Dobkins family for generations. I knew I would miss every inch of the place, from the huge stone fireplace in the living room to the comfy nook on the south side of the building with its window seat, just the perfect place to curl up on a winter morning with a good book.

Would I even be allowed time to read for pleasure while at the academy? I had no idea, since no one had given me any real details on what my next three years of training would even look like. It wasn't that unusual for a witch or wizard to pursue post-secondary education; my sister Rose was currently studying at the Phantasmagorical Institute in London, burnishing her skills at conjuring and transformation.

But that was very different from the sort of remedial school I would be attending, where probably the most I could hope for would be to learn enough control that I didn't leave a trail of shattered crockery, dead tomato plants, and high-flying cakes behind me.

My mother and I made our way through the house and out to the garage, a converted barn now given over to storage of the family vehicles. I had heard that in Mundania, those without magic burned something called petrol to power their cars and trucks and buses, but we had no need of such clumsy and dirty means to get around. Every vehicle in our world was powered by magic, by enchantments put in place by skilled witches and wizards at an elegant factory. Every year—or every other year, depending on how expensive the vehicle had been to begin with—we had to take our cars in for a recharge, so to speak, but that was the only maintenance they required.

I opened the rear hatch of the shiny silvery vehicle my parents had bought only the year before and deposited my suitcase inside. It seemed strange to have a single piece of luggage for a sojourn that would last for three years, but those had been the instructions. I had five changes of uniform, and was allowed to bring along three personal outfits and no more.

Why I would even need that much, when it seemed as though I would be spending every waking hour being put through my paces at the academy, I didn't know. But in addition to the uniforms, I had packed two pairs of trousers and two shirts and jumpers, and then my favorite fancy dress, the green velvet one with the gracefully draped neckline. I suppose I thought I might wear it to a midwinter celebration…assuming Miss Primm allowed such festivities at all.

Well, I would find out sooner or later. There was still so much I didn't know about where I was going.

My mother had already gotten in the driver's seat, so I went around to the other side of the car and climbed in. At once, I felt the invisible embrace of the protective spell put in place to ward off any injury in the unlikely event of an accident. Again, that was something that had been set up at the factory, although that enchantment had to be recharged every once in a while as well.

"Drive," my mother said aloud, and the car backed itself out of the garage and pointed itself toward the narrow lane that connected our property with the main road.

Miss Primm's academy was located in the south of England, not so very far from the home where I'd grown up, although the drive would still take an hour or so. I suppose our vehicles could have been enchanted to go faster, but in my world, no one was ever in too much of a hurry. I had heard that in Mundania, the magic-less people there often had to work forty hours a week or even more to maintain their lifestyles, but we were not so constricted. People had careers, of course, but in general, their work never required more than half that amount of time in a single week, and sometimes far less. My father worked rather more than that, but then, he had a highly specialized and necessary position.

If I were ever able to actually gain control of my magic, I would have to decide what I wanted to do with the rest of my life. While I admired my mother's mastery of domestic magic, that seemed a rather tame way to spend one's existence. Perhaps I would discover that I had powers similar to my father's, and would go to work for DOME, just like him.

Then again, I wasn't sure whether I would really enjoy doing that sort of work. It seemed a terrible thing to exile those without magic, even though I had been told since I was a very small child that the only reason our society functioned as well as it did was because everyone contributed magically. A person without any powers—or with powers they couldn't control—would be the worst sort of liability.

Because it had seemed increasingly likely during the course of my secondary studies that I might suffer that very fate, I had read more about DOME and its work than probably most. Children's powers started to show at a young age—usually around four or five. If those magical talents didn't appear, then the child would be evaluated by those trained to detect whether an individual had any magic at all, or whether they were what was commonly referred to as "soul dark"—without the spark of magic that made us all who we were. Those poor children were taken from their families and sent to Mundania, to be adopted there. One might say this was cruel, but part of DOME's standard procedure was to cast spells that erased all memory of living in a world with magic.

After all, it was hard to long for something you couldn't even remember.

Even so, I tried not to shiver at the thought I

might suffer the same fate. It was more difficult to cast the enchantments that sent a person in their late teens or early twenties to Mundania, simply because they had far more memories to remove, but it was something the agents at DOME were forced to do from time to time. I could always tell the days when my father had been involved in such an activity, because he looked somehow heavy of spirit, the weight of what he had to do for his work bearing down on his broad shoulders.

Both my mother and I were silent during our drive to the academy. I believe she wanted to give me room to think about what awaited me at Miss Primm's…or possibly she'd realized she had run out of reassuring words. It had to be difficult for her as well, to be taking me to a place from whence I might not return.

Because that was the worst of it. At the end of each year, all students at Miss Primm's had to undergo a series of final examinations to prove they had mastered the skills they'd been taught during the preceding months. Those who failed those tests were immediately sent off to Mundania—no chance to say goodbye or to gracefully close out their affairs. Actually, I had the notion that was part of the reason the students weren't allowed to go home for any kind of holiday…they would already be emotionally and mentally separated from their families.

I told myself I wouldn't suffer that fate. After all, Great-Grandmother Fern had survived the ordeal, and so should I.

Despite those inner reassurances, my heart began to pound as we turned off the highway and onto the gravel road that led to the academy. When it came into view—a gracious Georgian manor house, with a façade of warm-hued stone and coolly classical pillars framing the entrance—my pulse accelerated its pace. I had seen pictures of the place, of course, but it looked so much more intimidating in person.

The car came to a smooth stop next to the flagstone walkway that led to the front door. I knew this would be the most difficult part, for I would have to say goodbye to my mother here in the car. No one except students and staff were allowed on the grounds, except for this brief space of time when we were being dropped off.

Before I could say anything, my mother reached over and gave my hand a brief, fierce squeeze. Good thing Flo and Sam had decided to sleep through the ride in my sweater pockets. "You can do this," she said. "I believe in you, Calendula."

That she'd used my given name rather than the nickname I'd gone by since I was a very little girl signaled the gravity of the situation. I made myself smile, even though it felt as though I was stretching my mouth into a grimace.

"Thank you, Mother," I replied. Being careful not to squish my sleeping gerbils, I leaned over and gave her a quick hug, even though we weren't usually a demonstrative family.

Then again, this situation wasn't quite what one could call normal.

Her arms tightened around me, and then she pulled away. Her gaze moved forward, to look through the windscreen, and I could tell she was already trying to put some distance between us in order to lessen the hurt. "It will be fine. Make sure you write."

"I will," I promised. At least we were allowed that much. Letters could go back and forth freely between students and their families and friends, even if we couldn't have visitors. "I'll write as soon as I have something interesting to tell you."

"Write me even if you don't." My mother blinked. Was that a glitter of tears in her eyes?

I told myself the shimmer I'd seen was only a reflection from the car windows. Right then, I didn't want to acknowledge that my mother might be crying...or I'd start crying, too, and would look a horrible mess when I made my entrance.

"Absolutely," I said, then forced myself to push open the door and get out. I went around to the back and extricated my suitcase before closing the trunk lid. Even as I raised my hand in farewell, the car began to pull away.

Well, that was it. Now there was only one thing I could do.

I squared my shoulders and headed toward the academy's entrance.

CHAPTER 2

DINNER AT SIX

A s soon as I entered the building that housed Miss Primm's academy, a brisk little wind approached me, saying, "Calendula Dobkins?"

"Callie," I replied automatically.

The wind made a *tsk*-ing noise, then said, "You are in Room 212. Up the stairs there, and halfway down the hall to the right. Supper is promptly at six."

After delivering that information, the wind took itself off, disappearing down the ground-floor corridor that appeared to bisect the building. I wanted to shake my head, but it wasn't that odd an enchantment. Actually, it made sense to greet the students this way, rather than force one of the instructors to take on such a duty.

The staircase was directly in front of me, a

grand curve of steps with a wrought-iron balustrade. Underneath my feet was a floor of patterned marble, and high above, the ceiling spanned a huge arch, painted with frescoes of clouds and flocks of flying birds.

Before this, I'd only seen images of the exterior of the school, and so I wasn't quite prepared for the grandeur I saw around me. Honestly, the place looked like the manor house of a wealthy lord or lady, not a school for witches who couldn't manage their talents. Surely a great deal of effort must be expended at all times to keep the interiors looking so pristine.

Time for those ruminations later, however. I tightened my grip on my suitcase and walked over to the stairs, marveling at how quiet my surroundings seemed to be. The number varied from year to year, but there were generally somewhere around eighty or ninety students at the school at any given time. With that many girls between the ages of eighteen and twenty-one sheltered under a single roof, one would think the place would be a bit noisier.

Then again, the brisk little wind that had greeted me had made it sound as though I was expected to stay in my room until it was time for supper. I guessed everyone else was in their rooms already, waiting for the appointed time.

The upstairs hall was quite grand as well, with

an intricately woven rug nearly covering the gleaming wooden floor, and sconces that glowed with fairy light set at regular intervals along the walls, which were painted a soft shade of coral. Just as the wind had said, Room 212 was in the middle of the hallway on the righthand side.

Should I knock? I knew that we were all expected to have roommates, and I had no idea whether the girl I'd be sharing Room 212 with had arrived at the academy yet.

Better to be safe, I suppose.

I lifted a hand and knocked. Almost at once, a girl's voice said, "Come on in!"

Was that an American accent?

I didn't know why I should be surprised. After all, students came to Miss Primm's from all over the world, not just England.

Trying to arrange an unconcerned expression on my face—and not sure how successful I was—I opened the door with my free hand and let myself in. I got a brief glimpse of a room with high ceilings ornamented with plaster detailing and a tall window framed by soft blue drapes, before I focused on the girl standing by one of the beds.

Like me, she wore the school uniform of a red cardigan, plaid skirt, and white blouse. However, she had the most amazingly curly brown hair that surrounded her face like a cloud, and brown eyes and smooth brown skin. Smiling, she said, "I'm Juno Hightower," and stuck out her hand.

I'd never had a girl offer to shake hands before, but perhaps they did things differently in America. Trying not to look as though I'd hesitated, I took her hand and gave it a single brisk pump, and hoped that was correct etiquette. "Callie Dobkins," I replied, then added, "I'm a first."

"Me, too," Juno said. "I think they make sure to put us together with people from our same year."

That made sense. We'd be in the same classes, trying to surmount the same hurdles. "Have you met anyone else yet?" I asked.

She shook her head, setting that extraordinary mane of curls bouncing. "Nope," she said, although she didn't appear too disappointed by that lack. "That chatty little wind sent me straight up here. You?"

"The same," I responded before setting down my suitcase. Flo and Sam poked their heads out of my pockets to take a look around as I straightened.

"Ooh!" Juno exclaimed. "Are those your familiars?"

"Yes. The ginger one in my right pocket is Jetsam, and the mostly white one on the left is Flotsam." I paused then and took a quick look around the room. As far as I could tell, I didn't see any sign of an animal that could be Juno's familiar.

She seemed to guess what I was up to, because she grinned and went over to the window, then cracked it and let out a sharp whistle. Almost at once, a bright green and turquoise bird flew in and landed on her shoulder. "This is Fred," she said.

"He's lovely," I said, which was only the truth. The little bird's brilliant plumage was a splash of the tropics in that proper English room.

"To look at," Juno responded, mouth curling slightly. "Sometimes he can be a real pain."

"Be a real pain, be a real pain," Fred squawked, and I couldn't help but laugh outright.

"Did you teach him to do that?"

She raised a hand to her shoulder and extended her index finger, and immediately the little budgie climbed on and ruffled his feathers slightly. "No," she said. "He's just an amazing mimic. I have to be careful what I say around him, because otherwise he'd be repeating all kinds of awkward stuff."

"I wish I had a familiar that talked," I said, even as Flo gave an indignant shake and crawled her way out of my pocket, pulling little snags in my sweater with her sharp claws.

"You say that now," Juno remarked. She took

Fred over to the window and let him hop off onto the sill, then went to the room's single closet and pulled out a pretty little rounded cage. After putting it down on top of one of the room's two dressers, she added, "It's not so fun when you can't get them to shut up."

I suppose I could see how that might be a problem. Still, if nothing else, I liked the idea that her familiar was so different from mine. Flotsam and Jetsam were extremely easygoing little animals, and so I doubted they would have a problem with having Fred around.

The bird obligingly climbed into his cage after Juno opened the door for him, and so I thought it was time to get the gerbils settled as well. I picked up their cage from where it sat on the floor next to my suitcase and set it on the dresser that was currently unoccupied. Flo and Sam took the hint and scrambled inside, scratching around in the bedding to get comfortable.

I unhooked their water bottle and asked Juno, "Do you know where the bathroom is? I need to fill this up."

"No," she said cheerfully. "I got here only about five minutes before you did. But we can go exploring together."

Remembering the instructions from the wind that had greeted me, I replied, "Are you sure that's all right? I got the feeling we were supposed to stay in our rooms until supper."

Juno shrugged. "If someone catches us, you can just tell them we're getting water for our familiars. They can't expect us to let them die of thirst, right?"

This sounded sensible enough to me, so I nodded. She went over and unhooked the water bottle from Fred's cage, and the two of us ventured out into the hallway.

It was still empty…and quiet. I had to again wonder how a place that housed so many girls could be this silent, but perhaps the rooms were exceptionally soundproofed.

Or, considering the school was run by a mistress of magic, it seemed even likelier that some sort of spell had been placed on the students' rooms to ensure that the peace and quiet of the academy wasn't disturbed.

The silence made me want to keep quiet as well, but clearly, Juno didn't feel the same way. "So, what's your jam?" she asked, brown eyes glinting with interest.

"'Jam'?" I repeated, not sure what she'd meant. Clearly, it was going to take me a while to get used to her American slang.

She grinned. "I mean, what landed you in here? Hardly any magic, or magic out of control?"

Recalling the way that birthday cake had

flown around my mother's kitchen, I couldn't do much except smile in return. "Magic out of control," I said. "It's strong enough, but it doesn't do what I want."

That admission earned me a sympathetic nod. "I feel ya. Like, I'm the queen of opposites. I think I'm performing a spell correctly, and it always does the total reverse."

"Oh, that has to be annoying." I paused by a door that stood partway open, then peered inside, seeing a long row of sinks topped by individual mirrors against one wall. "I think this is the loo."

Juno's mouth quirked at that peculiarly British word, but she didn't say anything, only pushed past me to enter the bathroom. As I'd noted just a moment earlier, there was a row of ten sinks on one side, with a row of toilet stalls immediately facing the sinks. Around a corner was a set of showers—each of them enclosed with opaque glass, thank goodness. I'd never lived in a dormitory before and hadn't been looking forward to putting myself on display around all the other girls on my floor.

Luckily, it didn't appear that would be too much of a problem.

I filled up the gerbils' water bottle, then said, "Have you ever tried performing a spell in reverse? That is, saying it in a way that's the opposite of

what you want, so you'll get what you were originally aiming for?"

Juno turned the tap at the sink next to mine
and began filling Fred's bottle. "Yep. Doesn't
work. It just does something the opposite of what
I'm saying, but not what I would have wanted it
to do. Total mess."

"I'm sorry."

Her shoulders lifted, and she reached for the
tap and shut it off. "Yeah, it's a royal pain. But
that's why we're here, right? To get all our magical
troubles fixed?"

That was the theory. Three years of rigorous
training at the hands of Miss Primm and her
capable teachers, and we would all be set right and
ready to make our own ways in the world.

But had they ever dealt with students who
sounded as hopeless as Juno and I?

Of course they have, I told myself, using a
brisk inner voice that brooked no nonsense. *This
academy has been helping witches like you for
more than two hundred years. Do you honestly
think you're the worst witch to ever enter these
halls?*

Put that way, the situation didn't seem quite as
dire. "Precisely," I said as I also shut off the water.
Some of it had dripped on my fingers, but that
was no real problem. I wiped them on my skirt
and added, "I suppose we'd better get back."

"To take care of our thirsty familiars," Juno said.

The two of us headed out into the hallway. We'd only gone a few steps when an austere-looking woman with iron-gray hair and a severely cut black skirt suit appeared out of nowhere in front of us, her arms crossed.

"Just what do you two think you're doing?"

Juno and I exchanged a glance. Technically, we were both adults and could do as we pleased, since we were eighteen. However, by attending the academy, we'd handed over some of our independence in exchange for receiving the tutelage we so desperately needed. It made for a rather awkward situation, to say the least.

Probably better to err on the side of caution. Besides, we'd only been taking care of our familiars. Surely even this iron-faced woman couldn't fault us for that.

"Fetching water," I said, raising the bottle I held. Next to me, Juno did much the same thing. "We didn't want our familiars to go thirsty."

Not even a blink. "There was bottled water waiting for you in the wardrobe in your room—or did you not bother to look?"

Well, of course we hadn't. Then again, it wasn't as though a wardrobe generally tended to be the sort of place where one would look for water, so I thought Juno and I could both be forgiven our oversight.

"No, we didn't," Juno said. I had a feeling that I probably looked far too guilty, but she wore a half smile and didn't appear put off by this apparition at all. "Sorry about that."

"Well, go on back to your room," the woman said. "Take care of your familiars, but don't come down to the dining hall until six o'clock."

Having delivered that command, she disappeared into thin air just as abruptly as she had arrived. I blinked at the spot where she'd been standing.

"Nice trick," I said, once I knew Juno and I were safely alone. "I wish I could come and go that easily."

"No kidding," she replied. "My mother can manage it without even breaking a sweat, but I know better than to try. I'd probably end up on the moon or something."

That image made me want to laugh, although I knew that if such a thing were to happen in real life, Juno would be in very dire straits…unless she could use a spell to conjure herself a space suit. Since she didn't seem to have any more control over her magic than I did, the likelihood of such a thing happening was probably not very high.

We returned to our room and took care of our respective familiars. It did seem that Flo and Sam were getting along well enough with Juno's budgie, although Fred kept shooting them wary glances, as if he still wasn't quite sure what to make of his new furry roommates.

I, on the other hand, was more than pleased to have Juno sharing my dormitory room. Yes, we'd only just met, but she was certainly far friendlier than any of the girls I'd gone to school with—probably because she was just as hopeless at being a witch as I.

Misery loved company, after all.

While we waited for six o'clock to roll around, we chatted about our families. Juno was an only child, with parents who both worked in the publishing industry. I thought it was quite amazing for them to be involved in the production of books and the animated stories they contained, but she didn't seem too impressed.

"They don't *write* the books, after all," she said. "They only own a publishing company."

I still thought that owning a publishing company sounded quite grand. However, since Juno apparently was jaded by proximity to her parents' work, I tried not to be too effusive.

"Well, it still sounds more exciting than having a father who works for DOME," I said, and Juno's big brown eyes widened even further.

"Your father is with the Department?" she asked. "That must be...scary."

That was one word for it. Most of the time, I tried not to think too much about my father's work, and how one day he—or at least someone he knew well—would be responsible for banishing his youngest daughter from the magical world.

If I failed, of course.

I shrugged, and sipped some water. Since we'd already gotten water for the familiars, Juno and I had dipped into the bottled stuff we'd found in the wardrobe. "He doesn't talk about it much," I said. "Which is probably for the best." Then, thinking I should change the subject, I added, "Who do you think that woman was? Miss Primm?"

Juno had been playing with one of her curls, pulling it taut, then letting go so it would spring back into a perfect corkscrew spiral. She paused then, nose scrunching slightly as she considered my question.

"I don't know," she said after a pause. "Do you think the headmistress would be wandering around the halls, looking to bust random students for breaking the rules?"

Good question. It did seem like the sort of duty that might be delegated to one of the other teachers. Then again, the way the woman had appeared and then disappeared with such elegance spoke of someone very much in control of her magic. It was the kind of spell that many witches and wizards never mastered, and so I had to wonder if there were a number of faculty members other than Miss Primm who could pull off such a trick.

"Possibly," I replied. "If she wants to keep us all off guard."

Juno chuckled. "Well, I suppose we'll find out when we go down to dinner." A pause as she glanced over at the clock ticking on the wall, and then she added, "Thank the Source that it isn't too far off. My parents took me out for a burger before they brought me here, but I'm hungry."

"Were you staying in London?" I asked.

She nodded. "We took the TransAt, then stayed for a few days so we could explore. They tried to make it seem like a holiday, which was nice." The cheerful light in her eyes faded, and she said, in a much soberer tone, "Still, I couldn't help thinking about what was going to come at the end of our little holiday."

I knew exactly how she must have felt. My own mother had done her best to keep me cheered up, making me my favorite meals, not asking me to help with chores, and yet I still couldn't escape the horrible fact that my life was going to change forever in a few short days. And I hadn't even had the exciting distraction of riding the TransAt—a magically powered fleet of airships that regularly traveled the North Atlantic—to keep me occupied.

"Well, we're all in pretty much the same boat," I said, hoping I sounded hearty and not at all discouraged. "That's the good thing. And really, far more people graduate from Miss Primm's than...well, than otherwise, so I don't see any reason why we shouldn't be counted among that number, too."

My words seemed to cheer Juno, because she sat up a little straighter on her bed and gave a vigorous nod, one that set all her curls bouncing. "Darn right. I mean, there are those who don't graduate, but they're definitely in the minority."

I reflected that there were probably scores of other girls in the building who were thinking much the same thing, but I didn't want to say those words out loud. No, we needed to go on reassuring ourselves, especially since the hard math was in our favor.

We were saved from any further speculation by the sound of a loud bell reverberating throughout the grand manor house. Juno raised an eyebrow.

"I assume that means it's time for dinner."

"It would seem so." I got up from the bed and smoothed my skirt, then ran my fingers through my hair. Probably, I should have brushed it, but there wasn't time to worry about that now. I had a feeling Miss Primm wouldn't look favorably on students who were late to their first supper at the academy.

The familiars had already been fed, so we hurried out of our room and found ourselves surrounded by a group of twenty or so other girls, all of whom appeared to be around our same age. Since the building had four stories, it made sense to me that all the students from a single year would be housed on the same floor. I suppose that the floor remaining would be devoted to class-rooms and housing for the faculty...unless they lived off site.

We were all casting curious glances at one another, but no one appeared inclined to intro-duce themselves, not when we had someplace we needed to be. I was just glad that I had Juno at my side and we were already on our way to being friends, or I probably would have been even more intimidated by that flood of humanity than I already was.

Everyone made their way to a large hall on the ground floor, one with more of those magnificent plaster-embellished ceilings, as well as long cloth-covered tables with benches set next to them. Since Juno was a bit taller than I was, I allowed her to push forward through the throng toward one of the tables near the back. It was already mostly full, but two places on one of the benches remained, and we both sat down quickly, glad that we wouldn't have to go in search of another spot.

At the far end of the hall was one long table with high-backed chairs set on one side only, facing the rest of the room. Most of those chairs were already occupied by an assortment of witches, among them the stern-faced woman who'd confronted Juno and me in the upstairs corridor.

My companion had obviously caught sight of her as well, for she nudged me in the ribs with one elbow and leaned her head toward the witch in question. About all I could do was nod in acknowledgment, letting her know she'd clearly been right about her not being Miss Primm herself, since the highest-backed of the chairs at the head table, the one placed in the dead center, remained empty.

No sooner had everyone sat down than a woman entered the room through a doorway to the left of that table. She wore a high-necked blouse with a large cameo pinned to the front, and her heavy dark brown hair was swept up into a quite showy pompadour.

"Good evening, ladies," she said. "I am Penelope Primm, the headmistress of this academy, and I will be overseeing your education for the next three years."

I tried not to stare at her in surprise. True, the

headmistress was dressed almost exactly how I'd imagined her, and that much fit my expectations. The woman herself, however, had turned out to be much younger than I'd imagined, with finely drawn, elegant features, and didn't seem to be much older than her early or middle thirties at the very most. Almost all of the witches sitting at the head table were definitely older than she by a decade or more.

Possibly the faintest hint of a smile touched her lips as she continued. "I know this is not the sort of academy a young witch dreams of attending one day. Indeed, the Academy for Wayward Witches is a last resort for everyone who attends this school, and so I shall not attempt to ignore your reasons for being here, nor sugarcoat the very difficult work we must undertake to ensure you graduate successfully. That said, however, I have no reason to believe that all of you will not finish your course of studies here and be ready to face the next stage of your lives as you become efficient practitioners of the magical arts. Tomorrow, you will embark on those studies. For now, though—" she paused, and I could have sworn I saw a cheerful glint enter her eyes, even though I was sitting too far away to guess what their color might be—"for now, enjoy this feast, and begin to make new friends."

Her speech concluded, she turned and went

around to the high table so she might take her seat. At the same time, carts laden with food began to roll on their own power in the aisles between the tables, pausing from time to time so those in close proximity could help themselves to all the delicacies offered.

I'd seen similar spells at work in the restaurants where my parents had taken the family to eat, although not quite on such a grand scale, nor with so much variety offered. When a cart stopped near Juno and me, I was able to fill my plate with roast beef and mashed potatoes, steamed asparagus, fresh-baked rolls, and apple compote, while Juno opted for roasted chicken and rice, as well as some kind of dish of squash and corn.

"I hope there's a good gym class, or I'm going to get fat if I eat like this every day," she murmured to me as she placed her napkin on her lap.

Much the same thought had been running through my own head. There hadn't been any mention of physical education as part of the curriculum at the academy, but I had to believe they would keep us physically active somehow, or otherwise all of us would be in trouble if we ate like this at every meal.

But worries about expanding waistlines disappeared as soon as I put the first bite of food in my mouth. My mother was a renowned kitchen witch, but the fare at Miss Primm's put her meals to shame. If I must get fat, at least I'd do so happily.

All around us, the other girls ate with good appetite as well. Possibly they weren't quite sure how to break the ice, either, although after we'd applied ourselves to our food for a few minutes, a black-haired girl with unfortunate brows tilted her head toward me and inquired, "Aren't you Calendula Dobkins?"

"Callie," I said, an automatic response. Then I stared at the strange girl with some curiosity, since I was sure I'd never seen her before, and I couldn't think of how she might have recognized me. "And you are?"

"Mona McGee," she replied. "My father works with your father at DOME. I've seen your picture on his desk."

This explanation made some sense, although I couldn't quite hold back an irrational stab of jealousy at her words. My father had never brought me to his office, telling me it was no place for a young girl. I'd accepted that excuse, even as I realized his reticence was probably due much more to my clumsiness as a witch than because there was anything going on at the DOME offices that needed to be shielded from his daughter's eyes.

But clearly, Mona's father had no such reservations, because he'd taken his daughter there and apparently had introduced her to his coworkers. My father had a private office, and so there would have been no reason for Mona to go inside other than to meet one of her father's fellow agents.

"Oh," I said vaguely, since I didn't quite know how to respond. Also, there was something about Mona that got my hackles up, despite having already admonished myself not to be intimidated by the other students, since none of them were exactly models of witchy talent. Then, because I didn't want to sound too ignorant, I added, "I gave him that photo last Midwinter. I'm glad he has it on his desk."

"It's a good image," Mona remarked. "You actually look quite pretty in it."

From those words, I gathered that I was somewhat lacking in real life. Before I could think of a suitable retort, Juno shifted in her seat next to me and said, "You know, Mona, if you've lost your tweezers, you can borrow mine. Just because we're all stuck in here with a bunch of other girls doesn't mean we shouldn't try to look our best if we can."

All around us, there was a silent chorus of widened eyes. The girl sitting next to Mona, who had white-blonde hair and brows as insignificant as Mona's were prominent, scowled at Juno. "*I* think her eyebrows are just fine."

Clearly unperturbed, Juno picked up the roll

from her plate, tore off a piece, and took a bite. "Just trying to help."

"Well, we don't need your help," the girl retorted.

Mona shot her companion an irritated glance, as if annoyed that she'd interceded on her behalf. Mouth tight, she announced, "I think this table doesn't quite suit me. Come on, Philippa."

The two of them got up and flounced off as best they could, considering they took their plates and glasses with them. An uncomfortable silence descended, one that at length was broken by a series of giggles.

"Did you see her face?" one of the girls sitting on the opposite side of the table asked. Her brown hair was pulled back in a sleek ponytail, and she spoke with a clear French accent, although her English sounded impeccable. "I thought she was going to burst a blood vessel!"

More giggles, and another girl, this one with big blue eyes and hair nearly as curly as Juno's, chimed in, "It would have been better for all of us if she had. I went to school with Mona McGee, and she's a nasty piece of work."

Everyone who'd overheard our exchange nodded, and I couldn't help feeling cheered by their response. Clearly, those two girls had already chosen sides…and it seemed they were on mine.

As dinner wore on, though, and I learned the

names of my table mates—Celeste Saint-Michel was the French girl, and Helen Jenkins the one with the curly hair—doubt began to creep in. It seemed I had some allies…for now at least…but I didn't much like the idea of gaining an enemy my very first day of school.

Unfortunately, there didn't seem to be much I could do about it.

My heart sank the next morning when I entered the classroom for my first real lesson at Miss Primm's academy and realized that our instructor was the same the stern-faced woman who'd scolded Juno and me for wandering the halls the day before without permission. True, things weren't quite as grim as they could be, since I had my friend with me— and I also received several encouraging smiles from Helen and Celeste, the girls who'd taken my side at dinner the night before.

Still, I thought it was rather rotten of fate to make that formidable individual my first teacher, rather than some of the others I'd seen sitting at the head table during dinner. Most of them had looked far friendlier, and not nearly as frightening.

"I am Professor Hendricks," the woman

announced. Like Miss Primm, she wore a high-necked blouse and plainly cut skirt, although there was no cameo or any other jewelry to soften the severe lines of her outfit. She stood in front of a blackboard and sent us all what looked like a highly disapproving stare.

Then again, I had a feeling that was her usual expression.

"In Beginning Spells, you will learn to forget everything you've already learned, since it is quite obvious that it hasn't been working for you." Professor Hendricks paused there, her cold gray eyes—nearly the same iron-gray as her hair—surveying us one by one, as if cataloguing our individual shortcomings. It might have been my imagination, but it felt as though that cool gaze lingered on me for a moment longer than anyone else.

Every muscle in my body wanted to stiffen. What if she called me out in front of everyone, made a special point of telling the class that I'd managed to break the rules before we'd even got truly started?

Relief pulsed through me as her gaze moved on, although I sat quietly in my seat and did my best not to react. At the desk next to mine, Juno shifted uneasily, and I wondered if Professor Hendricks had also skewered her with that gimlet stare.

"You are all here because your magic has failed you at some level," the professor continued. "This means that the techniques you've been previously taught simply aren't effective at managing your individual gifts. It is this school's responsibility to retrain each and every one of you so you can wield those talents to the best of your ability."

For the first time, I noticed Mona McGee sitting on the far side of the classroom, her faithful shadow Philippa Carmody—Helen Jenkins had told me the pale-haired girl's full name—sitting next to her. Both of them kept sliding Juno and me evil little sideways glares.

Clearly, that particular grudge wasn't going away any time soon.

Professor Hendricks paused there, bony hands resting on her hips. "Is there a problem, Miss McGee?"

At once, Mona sat up straight in her chair and assumed an expression of utter innocence—or at least, as innocent as anyone could look with such forbidding eyebrows. "A problem, Professor Hendricks?"

"It appears you have something in your eye," the professor observed. "Or at least, that is how it seems to me. Why else would you be squinting in such a manner?"

Juno's mouth twisted, and I could tell she was working very hard to hold back a peal of laughter.

Rustles of movement from the desks in our vicinity seemed to indicate that several of our classmates were experiencing much the same problem.

Mona faced forward, shoulders tight. Although I could no longer see her expression, I guessed she was none too happy with any of us.

"I'm sorry, Professor Hendricks," she said in a mealy voice quite unlike the hectoring tone she'd used on me the day before. "I suppose I must have gotten a speck of dust in my eye. It's nothing."

For a moment, the professor only continued to gaze at her, as if she thought her stare might be sufficient to see the truth in her pupil's mind. Perhaps it could. Reading minds was very difficult, however, and a feat that not many witches or wizards could manage—and thank the Source for that—but because Professor Hendricks had already proved she could appear and disappear with ease, it didn't seem implausible that she might also be able to read the thoughts of others. It would definitely be a handy skill for a professor to possess.

But then the professor said, "I'm glad to hear it." A pause, and then she pointed at Juno. "Miss Hightower, if you could come here, please?"

She'd phrased the words as a request, but no one in the room believed they were anything other than a command. Juno sent me a brief, worried glance before getting up from her seat. Her hair bounced in a nonchalant way as she walked toward the front of the classroom, but I doubted she was as carefree as she appeared.

Why had Professor Hendricks called on her first? Sheer bad luck?

Possibly. I also had to shamefacedly admit to myself that I was very glad I'd escaped notice…for the moment anyway.

"Miss Hightower," the professor said after Juno paused by the lectern. "Please tell the class precisely why you're here at Miss Primm's academy."

My friend didn't exactly squirm, but I could tell from the way she looked down at the floor and her fingers played with the hem of her pleated tartan skirt that she dearly wanted to be anyplace but the spot where she currently stood. However, her voice was clear enough as she said, "It's because my magic always does the opposite of what I ask it to do…ma'am."

The honorific sounded tacked on, as if Juno had realized at the very last moment that it probably wasn't a good idea to respond without at least attempting to seem polite. Professor Hendricks' head tilted ever so slightly, even as her mouth tightened, and I wondered if she planned to call my friend to task for her near-slip.

To my relief, though, the professor only said,

"And have you ever tried to get to the bottom of the problem?"

"Well, of course I have," Juno responded, her voice now almost indignant. Clearly, she didn't like the insinuation that the reason why her magic was in such a woeful state was because she hadn't done anything to improve it. "I've tried everything. Doing spells in opposites, doing them backward…meditating and visualizing and breathing exercises and all other kinds of crazy things that I thought might help. But it was all just a total waste of time."

"Oh, I wouldn't say that," Professor Hendricks told her. "If you've practiced meditating and visualizing, then you already have a better handle on your mind and how it works than you might believe. Let us start with something simple, shall we?"

Out of nowhere, she produced a pair of scarves, one blue and one green. She handed both of them to Juno, who took the squares of silk with obvious reluctance, sending them a dubious glance before she raised her chin so she could look back at the professor.

"You see those two scarves?" Professor Hendricks asked, which seemed like a very obvious thing to inquire.

However, Juno dutifully nodded. "Yes, ma'am."

"You feel the silk? You can confirm that they're real?"

Again, Juno nodded. "Yes."

"Very good. I want you to hold the scarves for a moment, Miss Hightower. Feel the silk under your fingertips. Memorize their colors, the way they're hemmed…how much they weigh. Now imagine what it would be like if they were both gone."

"'Gone'?" Juno echoed.

"Yes," Professor Hendricks said. "I want you to make those scarves disappear, Miss Hightower."

"Oh, I've never been able to do anything like that, ma'am," my friend responded. Hers was the sort of complexion that couldn't precisely go pale, but I could tell she was worried. "One time I tried to make a butterfly disappear, and instead, a flock of seagulls showed up in the classroom."

One of Professor Hendricks' dark gray brows lifted. It wasn't difficult to believe that she might be visualizing the havoc a flock of birds could cause in her pristine classroom. When she spoke, however, she sounded singularly unconcerned. "I very much doubt we'll have to worry about seagulls on this particular occasion, Miss Hightower. I am only asking you to think of what it would be like if those pieces of silk were no longer in your hands, and to hold that feeling in your mind as you recite the spell to make them disappear."

Juno pressed her lips together and didn't say anything. But since she wasn't in a position where she could refuse, she pulled in a breath and closed her eyes—closed them so tightly, I could see just the hint of a line in the smooth brown skin between her brows. Her mouth moved, but she must have said the words of the disappearance spell in an undertone, because I couldn't hear her.

One of the scarves she was holding disappeared.

At once, her eyes flared open, and she stared down at the hand that had until a second or two earlier held a bright green silk scarf. "I did it!"

"You did half of it," the professor observed. "You only made one of the scarves disappear, not both of them. Can you tell me why that happened?"

For a moment, Juno was silent as she appeared to ponder the question. Then an odd little dancing light entered her eyes, and she said, "I think it's because blue is my favorite color, and so part of me didn't want to let go of that one."

"Very good," Professor Hendricks said. "In this school, we want you to *think* about your magic, not merely memorize lists of spells. That may work for some, but here we have learned that our students approach magic differently, and so it is important for us to recognize that one size most definitely does not fit all." Her tone shifted, became even brisker. "So, now that you understand why the one scarf disappeared and the other did not, perhaps you can try again with the scarf remaining."

Juno nodded and closed her eyes again, and then murmured the words of the spell. Almost at once, the blue scarf that had been dangling from one hand winked out of existence. All around the classroom were murmurs of appreciation.

I couldn't help but be impressed. Was it really that simple? Was the true solution something as simple as teaching ourselves a new approach to magic, one not merely predicated on rote memorization, but also on focusing how magic made us feel?

"Excellent," said Professor Hendricks. "That is a very good start. You may return to your seat."

Looking like she wished to beam from ear to ear—but doing her best to keep her expression sober—Juno came back and sat down at the desk next to mine. I desperately wanted to lean over and ask her exactly how she'd managed it, but I doubted that whispering in class was something the professor would tolerate.

I had to settle for sending my friend the quickest of sideways smiles, then sat and watched as Professor Hendricks called up one student after another, and had them attempt similarly simple magical feats. Most were able to acquit themselves well enough, although Helen Jenkins caught the edge of the professor's skirt on fire when she was only trying to turn out the lights overhead. This mishap didn't cause quite as much of a commotion as one might have thought, since Professor Hendricks didn't even blink as she waved a hand at her skirt, and at once the fire was extinguished as if it had never been.

"We will continue to work on control," she said smoothly, while a blushing, flustered Helen returned to her seat, hands visibly shaking.

"I never set anything on fire before," she muttered as she sat down.

Across the room, Mona McGee was smirking. The smirk disappeared with alacrity, however, as Professor Hendricks called her name.

"So, Miss McGee," the professor said once Mona stood next to her. "Tell us about your magical difficulties."

Spotty red color flared in Mona's cheeks. Clearly, she didn't much like having to confess her weakness in front of everyone. "It just…doesn't work," she said in a low voice.

"Doesn't work how, precisely?" the professor asked in carrying tones, and Mona flinched.

"There just doesn't seem to be much magic," she said. "I've managed a few very small, very simple spells, but when I try to do anything too difficult, it just doesn't happen."

"Ah," Professor Hendricks said. "Sometimes, lack of magic is nothing more than lack of desire."

Mona blinked up at the professor. "I don't understand."

The older woman's mouth thinned in what I thought was supposed to be a small smile, although it looked more like a grimace to me. "Did you truly want to cast those spells?"

"Well, of course I did," Mona replied, now looking indignant. "Why on earth wouldn't I want a spell to succeed?"

Her tone was anything but polite, and all around, it was as though we watching students held our collective breaths, wondering how Professor Hendricks would respond to such rudeness.

When she spoke, however, she sounded oddly mild. "As to that, Miss McGee," she responded, "only you can know for sure. Perhaps it wasn't a spell that interested you. Perhaps your mind was occupied with other matters. Perhaps…perhaps you didn't think it was terribly important."

"I always think these things are important," Mona said. She still looked flushed, but I got the feeling she was doing her best to moderate both her tone and her expression so she wouldn't irk the professor. "After all, my father works for DOME. I know what the consequences are if I don't succeed."

If she'd thought such a revelation would move Professor Hendricks, it seemed Mona was quite mistaken. The professor's stern expression hadn't shifted even a fraction of an inch. Then again, I suppose the professors at Miss Primm's would have acquainted themselves with our backgrounds so they would know what they were getting themselves into. Very likely, Mona's comment about her father hadn't been a surprise at all.

"Very good, then," Professor Hendricks said. "Since you are so aware of these consequences, then I think it would do well for you to keep them in mind as you work this next spell." She held out a hand, and on her outstretched palm, a small clay flowerpot appeared. "Buried inside the earth within this pot, Miss McGee," she went on, "is a single seed. I want you to make that seed turn into the daisy it is meant to be."

Mona's mouth opened slightly—perhaps to protest. But then she shut it again without speaking, and gave a single nod. Her eyes closed tight as she appeared to focus on the task the professor had given her, lips moving slightly as she uttered the words of the spell.

The room was so silent, I could probably have heard a mouse tiptoeing its way along the aisle next to my desk. Of course, I saw no such thing, probably because the elegant Miss Primm would never allow even a single stray rodent to disrupt her orderly school.

I watched the small red clay pot in Professor Hendricks' hand, expecting a green shoot to emerge from the soil within and then burst into a circle of white petals...but nothing happened. At length, Mona let out an angry gust of a breath.

"I tried," she said. "I *did.* I thought of the flower, and thought of what would happen to me if I couldn't make it grow and bloom. But nothing happened."

"Yes, I can see that," the professor observed dryly. "But we at Miss Primm's academy do not give up after only one attempt. Please try again."

Mona's lower lip began to form itself into a pout...until she realized that pouting was perhaps not the best way to ingratiate herself with Professor Hendricks. Almost at once, her mouth flattened into a thin line, and she closed her eyes once again.

Although I certainly wasn't what you could call invested in Mona McGee's success, I still found myself almost holding my breath, watching the innocuous-looking flowerpot as if it were an incendiary device loaded with fireworks spells, something that might go off at any second.

Unfortunately, it did not.

After a long, uncomfortable moment, Professor Hendricks said, "Perhaps you should take your seat, Miss McGee. We need to move on to another student, but never fear—we will revisit this later on. In the meantime, I think it's wise if you work on your concentration and motivation."

The heavy black bars of Mona's brows drew together, but even she wasn't quite brave enough to protest the professor's orders. Chin held high, she walked back to her desk next to Philippa and sat down, still staring defiantly at no one in particular.

If it had been someone else, I might have felt sorry for her. As it was, I could only reflect that I would rather have my own unruly gift than Mona's apparent lack of one.

Naturally, it was in that exact moment when Professor Hendricks called my name.

"Calendula Dobkins."

I startled, even as Juno shot me an encouraging smile. Well, easy for her to be encouraging; she'd acquitted herself very well this morning.

However, I managed to muster an answering smile before I got up from my desk and made the long walk to the front of the classroom. As I went, I couldn't help wondering what this place had been in a former lifetime. The academy had been founded just around two centuries earlier, but the building was much older than that. Had this room once been a parlor, or a grand banquet hall? Perhaps a ballroom?

Allowing those thoughts to occupy my mind helped me reach the spot where Professor Hendricks stood without making an utter fool of myself. Once there, I paused a pace or two away and did my best to look alert and eager, and not as though I very much wished I had the power to transport myself far away from here—perhaps to a canal boat in Venice, or atop a mountain in the Swiss Alps.

Unfortunately, I didn't possess anything near the skill to accomplish such a feat. About all I could do was stand there and hope that, whatever the professor asked of me, it wouldn't result in my blowing out all the windows or causing the ceiling to turn into pudding.

Since Professor Hendricks was staring at me, I stammered, "C-Callie, please, ma'am."

She didn't respond right away, only continued to bestow that frosty glare upon me. I half expected her to tell me that nicknames were all very well and good in the privacy of our families, but Miss Primm's was much more formal than that.

To my relief, she did not. She still held the flowerpot in her hand. "Miss Dobkins, let us see if you can manage what your classmate could not."

Oh, dear. I didn't think it would be a very good idea to show up Mona McGee by succeeding where she had failed, but I also didn't see how I could possibly refuse the professor's request.

Then again, I was rarely successful at these sorts of things, so I thought possibly I was getting ahead of myself.

"You want a daisy to grow?" I asked.

Her lips thinned. No doubt, she wasn't terribly impressed by my obvious stalling tactic. "Yes, Miss Dobkins," she said, clearly enunciating each syllable. "A single daisy, from the seed planted in the earth within this pot. Nothing fancy—this is our first day, after all."

I swallowed. She made it sound easy enough, but I knew better. I would have to think about that seed, consider the burgeoning life within it, and direct that energy outward so the seed would send out roots first, followed by a slender stalk to burst forth from the soil, and then at last the cheerful face of a daisy.

Well, I would just have to see what I could do. In the past, the few times when I'd actually been successful using magic, I hadn't even truly focused on what I was doing, had simply let whatever I was trying to do happen naturally. The problem was, when I tried to duplicate those results, I began to focus, and that appeared to be a recipe for disaster.

So…how to focus without *actually* focusing?

I didn't quite know the answer to that conundrum. All I could do was stand there and do my best not to think about the flower I was trying to conjure. Of course, the more I tried *not* to think about it, the more I did.

A muffled gasp swept over the classroom. Yes, there was a green shoot emerging from the pot… but then there was another, and another. Writhing tendrils of vines wriggled their way out of the pot, more and more of them until the clay itself gave way, shattering in an explosion of terra-cotta shards and dark brown earth. None of the debris seemed to touch Professor Hendricks, making me think she'd thrown up a protection spell at the last minute to shield herself.

But the vines kept coming, more and more of them, winding across the floor, moving toward the desks where my classmates sat. A few frightened shrieks, and the girls in the front row hastily climbed onto their seats, trying their best to avoid the writhing mass. The vines wound themselves around the legs of the chairs, and suddenly, more and more of my classmates were up off the floor, jumping from desk to desk in an attempt to avoid getting caught by one of the rogue vines.

"Enough," the professor pronounced. She murmured a few words under her breath, and in the next moment, all the vines I'd summoned began to shrivel and die, dwindling even as I looked. Within a moment, they had shrunk down to almost nothing, and in the next second, shivered into dust and disappeared.

I stared, wondering how on earth she'd managed such a feat.

Professor Hendricks turned toward me, her expression so neutral, I knew I was probably about to get a terrible dressing-down.

"Well," she said, "you certainly are very strong, Miss Dobkins. We shall have to work on control, however." And since I still stood there, not sure how I should respond, she made a whisking motion with her hands and added, "Back to your seat with you. I think you've done enough for one morning."

Filled with relief, I hurried to my desk and sank down in the chair. June sent me a quick glance, eyebrows raised, the look in her eyes one of respect.

I wasn't sure I'd earned that respect. True, even Professor Hendricks had commented on the strength of my magic, but what good was it if every spell I attempted went so horribly awry?

Well, it was only the first day. I had to hope that matters could only improve from here.

CHAPTER 4
GETTING FAMILIAR

To my relief, Professor Hendricks' class proved to be the most difficult one on my schedule, and the rest of the day went more smoothly. After two hours in Beginning Spells, our group moved on to Focus & Meditation, where we didn't do much except a series of breathing exercises. Juno seemed very happy with the coursework, probably because she'd already done that same sort of thing back home in America.

"A whole hour of just breathing and meditation?" she said as we trooped with the rest of the students toward the dining hall. "Sign me up! I think the hardest part for me was trying to stay awake—I didn't sleep very well last night. New bed, I guess."

I could understand that, since I'd found

myself tossing and turning, too. Not because the
bed wasn't comfortable, but because I'd been fret-
ting about what my first day at Miss Primm's
would be like. Having survived Professor
Hendricks' class—if just barely—I felt a bit better
about life.

And yes, I'd found my eyelids drooping once
or twice during the breathing exercises, but I'd
blinked vigorously and somehow managed to
prevent myself from rolling right out of the lotus
position that Professor Chopra, the Focus &
Meditation teacher, had told us we all had to
adopt while in her class.

"How on earth did you manage all that with
the vines?" Helen Jenkins asked as she settled
herself across the table from us. She sounded
almost envious, although I didn't know why
anyone should be jealous of my ability to make
aggressive greenery invade a classroom.

"I don't know," I admitted. The serving cart
stopped by us, so I had to pause to place a small
bowl of cut fruit and a large piece of quiche on
my plate before I could continue. "That's the
entire problem. The magic is there, but I can't ever
seem to make it do what I want."

"At least you didn't set Professor Hendricks'
skirt on fire," she said morosely. Next to me, Juno
barely held back a snicker.

Celeste had come along right then, and went

ahead and seated herself next to Helen. "Ah, well, there's always tomorrow," she remarked, clearly having overheard our conversation, and the rest of us chuckled.

"Truer than you know," I said as I stabbed a mandarin orange with my fork.

The look Celeste sent me then was almost pitying. Like Juno, she'd done fairly well in Beginning Spells, and had been able to change the color of a piece of fabric Professor Hendricks handed her from red to blue. True, the professor had requested that she turn it yellow, but at least it hadn't exploded or tried to turn our classroom into a replica of the Parthenon.

Juno said, "Still, at least you have magic, Callie, unlike...."

The words trailed off as she gave a significant nod toward the spot where Mona was sitting with Philippa, two tables over. They had their own little group with them, girls whose names I didn't know. Judging by the way they glanced over at me and my friends, I guessed there wasn't much chance that our two little "teams" would ever be friendly.

Which, I told myself, was fine. Because I really hadn't had any friends in school before this, I was now more than content to have as many as three. Perhaps I was being a bit presumptuous in thinking of Celeste and Helen and Juno as friends, since we hadn't known each other for very long. On the other hand, they definitely were cordial, which was more than I could say about the girls at my previous school.

"It's definitely better to have too much than none at all," Celeste put in, and gave Helen an encouraging smile. "So yes, you did set the professor's skirt on fire, but you had to have magic to do that, true?"

Hearing those words, Helen looked a bit cheerier, and she returned to her soup with a little more gusto than she'd shown previously.

Juno had gotten her class schedule out of her satchel and was studying it. "Working With Familiars is after lunch," she said. "And then it's Physical Activities, and finally Magical History. It looks like they're going to have us in class all the way until five." She wrinkled her nose and set the piece of paper down on the table. "Back in New York, I was done with school by three o'clock."

"Ah, but you had other things to do once school was over," Celeste pointed out. "It doesn't seem as if there is much to keep us occupied here except schoolwork."

I'd wondered about that. Even with being in one class or another until five o'clock, and presumably having some sort of homework to finish afterward, it didn't seem as if there was much provision to keep us occupied otherwise. Or possibly they expected us to practice our magic?

That didn't seem like the best of ideas. True, we were here to hone our skills, but considering the odds of a spell going awry, it seemed as though it was probably wiser to confine all our practice to the safety of the classroom, where one of the professors could step in if things got too out of hand.

"Well, there are the school grounds to explore," Helen said, and we all looked at her. She flushed a little at being the center of attention, but managed to go on, "Didn't you know? The academy sits on a piece of property that's almost three hundred acres in size. There's a pond and a forest, and even stables for riding."

"How do you know all that?" I asked. While I would be the first to admit that I wasn't the most dedicated student in the world, I'd studied the materials the academy had sent over once it had been determined I needed to attend. None of them had said anything about a forest or a pond, and certainly there had been nothing about stables.

Helen's cheeks went even pinker. "Because my mother attended here, too. She thinks it's all her fault that my magic is such a mess, since hers was as well."

"But she obviously graduated, right?" Juno asked.

A nod, although Helen didn't look particularly cheery about being able to answer in the affirmative. "Yes…barely. She's not a very gifted witch, but she can do enough to get by. Anyway, she told me about the grounds, about how there are places to explore and ride. Perhaps they'll tell us about the stables during the Working With Familiars class."

Possibly, although I didn't quite see how riding horses had much to do with managing a pair of gerbils—or a budgie, or whatever creatures my friends had as their familiars, since I had yet to see Celeste or Helen's companion animals. Still, it sounded like something fun to do; I'd never ridden a horse, but surely it couldn't be that difficult, could it?

"I wonder if they have horseback riding as sort of a reward or something," Juno remarked. She'd gotten herself a salad for lunch but didn't look too enthusiastic about eating it. "I mean, it doesn't sound like the sort of thing you need to get your magic figured out, does it?"

"It's part of Physical Activities," Helen told her. "At least, it was when my mother went here. I suppose they could have changed the contents of the course, but maybe we'll find out in class this afternoon."

I hoped so. I had to admit I was glad that Working With Familiars followed immediately after lunch, rather than PA. Running and jumping about generally wasn't recommended on a full stomach.

We were quiet for a while after that as we all attended to the meals in front of us. Soon enough, it was time to hurry upstairs to our respective rooms and fetch our familiars, since they weren't allowed in the other classes with us. Fred was rocking back and forth on the swing in his cage, calling out, "Flotsam and Jetsam, Flotsam and Jetsam!" over and over, while poor Flo and Sam sat in their own cage and stared at the budgie with puzzled eyes. They looked terribly relieved to be let out so they could wriggle into the pockets of my cardigan.

"Sorry about that," Juno said. She retrieved the voluble bird, scolding him, "Fred, you need to shut up."

"Shut up, shut up!" he repeated, bobbing his head this way and that.

Juno rolled her eyes. "I seriously don't know what I'm supposed to do with this darn bird. He's been like this ever since the day I got him."

"Well, maybe the Working With Familiars professor will have some pointers on that," I said, and Juno tilted her head slightly, considering my words.

"I hope so. Because this is getting old. I hate to think I'm going to be stuck with this idiotic bird bellowing whatever he wants for the rest of my life."

About all I could do was offer an encouraging smile. That was the thing with familiars—whatever a particular animal's life span might normally be, it was lengthened tremendously when it became a familiar. They bonded with their people and stayed with them until the day their person died, at which time they passed from this world as well. Some might say that was hard luck, but since my gerbils would—I hoped —get to stick around for eighty or so years rather than their usual three or four, I thought they were still probably getting the better end of the deal.

We joined up with Helen and Celeste as we headed down the stairs. Helen's familiar was a little banty rooster who kept trying to wriggle out of her arms, while Celeste's was a gorgeous Siamese cat with a sparkly pink collar. The cat eyed Fred, currently perched on Juno's shoulder, with the expression of someone who was sizing up a morsel and deciding whether it would be adequate to satisfy their hunger.

Obviously, Celeste was used to that sort of behavior from her familiar, because she tightened her grip on the cat and said, "Mignon is actually quite well-behaved. She just looks like she's contemplating murder."

"Good to know," Juno returned. "Although I'm not sure whether I'd be that upset if Fred ended up as a bedtime snack."

"Bedtime snack! Bedtime snack!" the budgie bellowed, and we all winced.

I knew Juno was joking. Witches and wizards formed very strong bonds with their familiars, and looked on them as family, so on the rare occasions when they were hurt or even killed, it was devastating to the humans they'd bonded with. Still, I thought I should count myself lucky that my own familiars were a couple of quiet little gerbils and not a squawking bird.

The Working With Familiars class was held in a gorgeous glass room that must have been the manor house's conservatory once upon a time. No desks here; trees still grew from expansive planters in the space, and the air was moist and scented with the perfumes of all the flowers that bloomed in pots beneath the trees. We stood in awkward little clumps, showing that we'd already formed our own cliques despite being at school for less than a day.

A tall woman with the most gorgeous red hair I'd ever seen strode into the space. Unlike Miss Primm and Professor Hendricks, who seemed to favor skirts, this woman wore slim black pants tucked into high boots, and an open-collared blouse, also black. A slender back ribbon encircled her throat, and at her side paced a large, rangy dog.

No, not a dog, I realized after a second glance. A wolf.

Murmurs ran through the crowd at the sight of the animal. Yes, some people had familiars that were wild animals—wolves, foxes, lions, panthers —but they were very rare. It was far more likely for your familiar to be a domesticated sort, like Celeste's Mignon or Helen's rooster.

The wolf didn't seem to pay any attention to the watching students, but only paced alongside his mistress until she came to a stop under a tree as slim and elegant as she was. "Good afternoon, everyone," she said. Her accent was from the south of England like my own, crisp and no-nonsense. "My name is Professor Hamilton, and I will be guiding you through Working With Familiars. I know that all of you are already…familiar…with your animal companions, and yet they can be so much more than mere companions. They can help you focus your magic, can be bell-wethers for the strength of your spells. They can offer protection, and guidance."

Next to me, Juno made a sound suspiciously like a snort. Clearly, she was having a hard time visualizing Fred as any kind of a protector. To be fair, I couldn't really see Flo and Sam coming to my aid in time of need, either. They were adorable and fun to have around, but I didn't exactly see them as stalwart warriors in defense of their mistress.

Either Professor Hamilton hadn't heard her, or she had decided that Juno's reaction wasn't worth a response. With no change in expression, she went on, "So, the first order of business is for you to introduce me to your familiars."

From there, she went up to each of us, inquired as to our name, and then asked us to tell her the names of our familiars. I was amused to see that Mona McGee's animal companion was a dubious-looking white rat; he didn't seem too happy to be there, but hung on to her shoulder and stared at the professor with blank red eyes when she walked up to meet him.

Once that business was managed, Professor Hamilton returned to her position under the tree, the big gray wolf still standing attention at her side. "Now, then," she said. "You have already had these familiars with you for years, but have you actually worked with them?"

We all traded uneasy glances. I had no idea what everyone else's experience had been, but because my own magic had been so unpredictable, both my parents and my teachers had advised me to look on Flo and Sam more as companions and friends rather than as anyone who could actually assist me with spell casting. My sisters worked with their familiars in various ways, using them as their eyes and ears when they weren't present, or having them help as a focus when they were casting spells, but I certainly hadn't done anything so ambitious with the gerbil pair who'd bonded to me when I was only five years old.

Judging by the way everyone maintained their silence, I got the distinct impression that their own experience had been much the same. To my surprise, Professor Hamilton didn't seem too put out by our lack of response. In fact, she smiled slightly, as if she'd been expecting that very thing.

"It's often easier for those around us to counsel caution when our magic isn't entirely reliable," she said next. "However, it is very important for you all to become comfortable working with your familiars. You know them well already, of course, because they have been a part of your lives for more than a decade. There's no need to fear—part of taking this coursework here at the academy should be the knowledge that we instructors are here to help you…and to put out any fires that may occur."

On my other side, Helen shifted uneasily. I could tell she was wondering if Professor Hamilton had heard about what happened to Professor Hendricks' skirt, or whether our current instructor had merely chosen an unfortunate turn of phrase.

"Callie Dobkins," Professor Hamilton said next.

My stomach sank, and I wondered if snagging a second piece of quiche at lunch had been such a good idea. Unfortunately, there wasn't much I could do about it now, although I really, really wished the professor had called on someone other than me. Being first was never fun.

Still, I knew that trying to demur—or pretend I was someone else entirely—probably wouldn't work very well in this particular situation. Doing my best to look calm and unconcerned, I stepped forward from the group and paused a few feet away from our teacher.

"Yes, Professor Hamilton?"

She still wore that half smile. Up close like this, I could see she had a few faint lines around her eyes and in the porcelain skin next to her mouth, but she was still so beautiful that I found myself wondering why she had chosen a life teaching magical misfits like myself rather than having a brilliant career in the outer world, or perhaps a family. True, I supposed it was possible she was married, and yet the setup at Miss Primm's academy seemed to preclude much of a personal life. Helen had already told us that all the professors had suites on the ground floor of the manor house, just as I'd surmised.

"Your familiars, Callie."

Well, at least she was calling me by my first name, rather than the formal "Miss Dobkins" form of address that Professor Hendricks seemed to prefer. I touched my pockets, where Flo and Sam had been hiding this entire time, and the pair of gerbils climbed out and perched themselves on my shoulders.

If Professor Hamilton was underwhelmed by my furry little companions, she showed no sign of her disappointment. I thought it was entirely possible that she'd known all about Flotsam and Jetsam before our little introductions at the beginning of class, since the names of my familiars and their species had been part of the information I'd been asked to include with my application to the academy.

"Flo and Sam," I said, quite unnecessarily, but it seemed as though I needed to say something.

"Excellent," Professor Hamilton returned. "They go everywhere with you, don't they?"

I nodded. I suppose that was one good thing about having such diminutive magical companions—they could easily ride along in a pocket or in a satchel, and could easily be concealed. You couldn't really say the same for a hawk, or a python…or a wolf.

The professor nodded. "Good. Then this may come more easily for you. I suppose you know how many people have their familiars work as their eyes and ears in places where they can't go?"

"Yes, ma'am," I replied.

"Have you ever tried to do that?"

"No," I told her. "Since they're with me all the time, I suppose I didn't see the point."

From behind me came the sound of muffled giggles, although I couldn't tell whether the suppressed laughter had my friends as its source, or Mona McGee and her cabal.

"And, no doubt, you were also told it wouldn't be safe to attempt such a thing."

I nodded. "That, too."

Professor Hamilton looked pleased. "I appreciate your caution, but, as I said earlier, we don't need to worry about that sort of thing here. I want you to send your familiars off to a different part of the conservatory, and then report on what they're seeing."

"How am I supposed to do that?" I asked, knowing even as I spoke how plaintive I sounded.

"By focusing on them, and on your connection to them," the professor replied. "It's really far simpler than you think. You already have a strong bond with your familiars, one that's been forged through all the years you've been together. All you have to do now is make it work for you."

I had my doubts, but I knew better than to voice them aloud. Instead, I told Flo and Sam, "Go exploring. Take a look around the conservatory."

When I was much younger, I'd wondered how my familiars could even understand what I was saying to them. But my mother had assured me that was all part of having a familiar, and sure enough, the two tiny creatures did seem to comprehend my comments and commands, even if we couldn't share anything that amounted to a real conversation.

Now, the two gerbils scampered down my arms, hung off the edge of my sweater for a second, and then dropped to the ground. After pausing for the barest second or two to get their bearings, they hurried toward the far wall of the conservatory.

Once again, the watching girls whispered amongst themselves, although I couldn't make out anything of what they were saying. Professor Hamilton ignored the rustle and said, "Now, Callie—tell me what your gerbils are seeing."

"I don't—" I began, and then stopped myself. This exercise was all about learning a new skill, flexing a muscle I'd never used before. It was only my first day at the academy, and yet I got the impression that phrases such as "I don't know how" and "I can't" weren't exactly popular around here.

So, the gerbils. In my mind's eye, I visualized them scurrying about, making their way past planters where trees and shrubs and even orchids grew. I saw Flo, nearly all white except for that one odd brown patch, and Sam, the same reddish brown all over, running along the cement-paved ground next to one another, pausing every once in a while to confer as to the best place to go in these unfamiliar surroundings.

They stopped under a plant I didn't recognize, one with long, sword-like fleshy leaves and a brilliant spiky bloom. It was quite striking, and so made a very good landmark.

"What are you seeing, Callie?"

I opened my eyes and saw Professor Hamilton watching with me with an expectant expression on her face, while my fellow classmates were likewise intently staring in my direction. Being the center of such attention was quite uncomfortable, but I tried to answer as honestly as possible.

"I'm seeing Flo and Sam sitting under some kind of flower or succulent," I replied. "It has a bright flower in a sort of coral-red shade, and the leaves are long and pointed, like a blade."

"I know the very one," Professor Hamilton said. "Let me go take a look."

She turned away from me and headed in the same direction the gerbils had gone only a moment earlier. I remained where I was, resisting as best I could the urge to knot my fingers in the plaid wool of my skirt as I waited nervously. What if I'd gotten it all wrong and had conjured the wrong image in my mind, my imagination coming up with a vision that had absolutely nothing to do with reality?

A few feet away, Juno shot me a grin and a thumbs-up, while Celeste and Helen also did their best to look encouraging. I knew that logically, there wasn't anything much for me to be worried about, since getting this visual connection with my familiars wrong wasn't quite the same thing as setting a bunch of wild vines free to wreak havoc in Professor Hendricks' classroom. All the same, I would prefer not to fail quite so spectacularly twice in a row.

Professor Hamilton returned a moment later, Flo and Sam riding on the shoulders of her shirt as if they'd done such a thing their entire lives. She paused next to me, and they hurried down her sleeves and leapt into my pockets, thus reassuring me that they still preferred my company, even if they hadn't scrupled to hitch a ride with my instructor.

"They were under the bromeliad, just as you described," she said. "That's excellent, Callie—I'm glad to see you already have such a strong connection with your familiars that you were able to use it to see their surroundings."

I wanted to sag with relief, but I only murmured a thank-you and then gratefully returned to my place next to Juno and Helen and Celeste.

After that, Professor Hamilton put everyone through their paces. I was glad to see that Juno acquitted herself well, clearly describing the branch where Fred alighted after she sent him flying about the conservatory. Likewise, Celeste showed that her connection with Mignon the Siamese cat was strong, too, since she saw immediately that he did not stay in the conservatory as commanded, but had tried to slink out through the door.

Poor Helen didn't fare as well; Ajax, her little banty rooster, flapped about, crowing, and did not seem to understand the command at all. Even when Professor Hamilton physically picked up the bird and deposited him elsewhere in the conservatory, Helen couldn't describe where he was, and had to have the professor go fetch him for her.

This incident made Mona McGee smile in derision. However, her lofty scorn didn't last very long, because she, too, seemed unable to establish any sort of connection to Silas, her rat, and he got himself so thoroughly lost that we ran out of time, and Professor Hamilton announced we would continue the lesson the next day.

"But excellent work for everyone who was able to complete the exercise," she added with an encouraging smile at Helen, who looked quite woebegone.

"An excellent mess," Helen muttered under her breath. She had Ajax tucked under one arm as we headed back to our rooms so we could get our familiars settled before heading out to Physical Activities. "I think I'm just as hopeless as Mona McGee."

I sent a worried glance around us, worried that Mona might have overheard. Luckily, the girl seemed so disgusted by her rat's performance that she'd hurried ahead of everyone, clearly wishing to get to her room as quickly as possible.

Juno patted Helen on the shoulder. "You're not hopeless at all," she said. "You're just having a bad day. Besides, you're not really like Mona, are you? I mean, you do have *some* magic, right?"

Helen's mouth was still drooping, but she appeared to perk up a bit at that question. "Some," she said. "I mean, I've managed a bit of magic here and there. But I never know when anything is going to work. There doesn't seem to be any rhyme or reason to it."

"That's still better than Mona," Juno responded. "I mean, she claims that she's gotten magic to work for her every once in a while, but she's batting oh-for-two here at the academy."

Helen, Celeste, and I traded puzzled glances. "Oh-for-two?" Celeste inquired.

Juno sent us all a pitying look. "It's a baseball term. Never mind. Anyway, all I'm saying is that Mona so far hasn't shown a single sign that she has any magic at all. It could be worse."

Helen appeared as though she wanted to protest, but by that point, we'd gotten to our floor and needed to go to our separate rooms to put our familiars in their various cages or pens. I petted Flo and Sam, and gave them each an extra treat. It seemed they'd earned that much for our excellent showing in the conservatory.

I knew I needed to hug that minor triumph to myself. After all, I had no idea whether I'd be able to repeat it in the days and weeks—and months —ahead.

We soon settled into a rhythm, becoming used to our daily schedule at the academy and the long days of magical work. I missed my family more than I wanted to admit—I'd hoped I would be a grown-up about the whole thing, and did my best to reassure myself that I didn't need my mother and father and could manage quite well on my own—but since all of us at Miss Primm's were in the same boat, it made this abrupt change in our lives a little easier to bear.

And I was more grateful than I wanted to say about my newfound friends. The four of us got along famously together, and I'd uttered a silent thank-you to the Source more than once for ending up with Juno Hightower as my roommate, and not Mona McGee. I honestly didn't know who had made that decision. Had Miss Primm determined all the room assignments, or was it done purely by lottery?

It was hard to say, for—despite attending her eponymous academy—we actually didn't see that much of the school's headmistress. She sat at the head table at every meal, true, but she didn't appear to teach any classes, and generally remained in her office at the north end of the building's ground floor, doing who knows what. From time to time, she would drop in to observe a class, an occasion that tended to engender extreme anxiety in whoever had the horribly bad luck to be demonstrating their magic—or lack thereof—in class whenever she chose to appear.

"Maybe she works more with the thirds," Juno remarked one day as we were speculating about the school's mysterious headmistress. Since it was a Sunday, we didn't have any classes, and were free to roam about the school's extensive grounds. And because it was a glorious day in early October, Celeste, Helen, Juno, and I had requested a picnic lunch of Miss Greenbriar, who ran the school's kitchen, and taken it to the pond Helen had told us about on our first day at the academy.

The four of us sat on a large blanket spread out on the grass, eating sandwiches and fruit and scones, and washing them down with ginger beer. A mild wind ruffled our hair, and our familiars prowled about, exploring the nearby territory. Even a few weeks earlier, I would have been worried about allowing Flo and Sam to go where they pleased, but now that I could see through their eyes and call them back whenever necessary, thanks to what I'd learned in Professor Hamilton's classes, I wasn't nearly so concerned.

Even Helen allowed Ajax to roam where he liked, since she'd finally managed to strengthen the bond between her and the little rooster enough that he would also obey her commands. He and Celeste's cat Mignon had formed an unlikely friendship, with the two animals often at each other's side, while Fred would flutter overhead.

At any rate, since our familiar creatures could take care of themselves, that meant we girls were free to gossip as we liked.

"Perhaps," Celeste said in response to Juno's comment, sounding a bit dubious. "Although I've spoken to several of the thirds, and they say she doesn't teach their classes, either."

"You talk to thirds?" Helen asked. Her big blue eyes widened. "When?"

"When I see them in the hallways," Celeste replied. Her expression was more amused than impatient; we were all used to Helen's shyness by that point. "They are students here, the same as the rest of us. Why shouldn't I talk to them?"

Helen remained wide-eyed. "I thought it wasn't allowed."

Both Juno and I chuckled at that statement. "I don't think it's so much about 'allowed,'" I said as I reached for another lingonberry scone. "I think it's more that our schedules don't overlap very much, and so we don't bump into each other all that often. Also, since the thirds' rooms are on a different floor from ours, there's not much opportunity for chatting."

"Celeste managed to," Helen returned, and I shrugged.

"I'm still surprised the headmistress is young and pretty," Juno said, apparently ready to abandon the topic of talking to the third-year students and go back to something she found far more interesting. She was leaning back on her elbows, the fingers of one hand idly wrapped around a bottle of ginger beer. "I was expecting some old prune."

We all chuckled at that comment. I had to admit I'd been expecting someone fairly prune-y myself, so I was always surprised on those rare instances when I caught a glimpse of Miss Primm. She had to be younger than all of her instructors by a decade or more.

Helen reached for an apple and took a bite. "This place has always been run by a Miss Primm. I suppose it's not so strange that she's not old.

After all, a new one has to take over at some point, right?"

"If she is even 'new' at all," Juno remarked, and we all stared at her.

"What are you talking about?" I asked.

She shrugged and swallowed some ginger beer. "Maybe some kind of magic is going on here," she said. "After all, has anyone ever heard of a *Mr.* Primm?"

We all pondered that question for a moment. "Well, no," I said. "But you don't need a husband to have a child, for goodness' sake."

My comment made Juno roll her eyes. "Of course not," she replied. "Still, wouldn't it make some sense that the original Miss Primm has been prolonging her life through magic?"

Celeste chuckled. "It is an interesting theory," she said. "But in the hall outside Miss Primm's office are a series of portraits of her ancestors, stretching back two hundred years. They do resemble one another, but it is also clear that they are not the same woman."

"When were you at her office?" Juno demanded.

I wondered the same thing. We all knew that Miss Primm's office was located on the ground floor of the enormous manor house that the academy now occupied, but as far as I'd been able to tell, no one went there unless expressly invited.

Unlike the other schools I'd attended, discipline here was managed by the individual professors. Then again, none of the students at the academy seemed inclined to misbehave, since we were all here voluntarily. Anyone who acted out ran the risk of being expelled...and therefore being granted an express ticket to Mundania, the one thing we were all trying very hard to avoid.

"Last week," Celeste said airily. "Professor Hamilton asked me to run a note over for her after class."

"And you didn't say anything to us about it?" Juno responded. Her brown eyes snapped with impatience.

"I did not see the need," Celeste said. With a shrug, she reached for a small bunch of grapes and popped one in her mouth. Somehow, she managed to be elegant even in jeans and a plain white shirt with the sleeves rolled up. Then again, she also managed to make her school uniform look like something off the runway in Paris, so I suppose I shouldn't have been too surprised. "Nothing happened. I went to her office and delivered the note, and then went on to Physical Activities. I noticed the portraits, but I didn't think they were all that important."

Juno listened to this account, a speculative light entering her eyes. "Hmm...so there are Miss Primms, but no Mr. Primm. I wonder how that works. Do you think each Miss Primm decides at some point to go off and have a torrid affair somewhere so she'll have a daughter to carry on the line?"

"When would she have the time?" Helen put in, looking perplexed, and we all laughed.

"Oh, there's always time for that sort of thing," Juno told her.

I wasn't so sure about that. We'd been informed that there was a small break in classes at the end of August every year, mostly to allow the professors to regroup after the end of the term— and presumably, after the thirds had either graduated to live a normal life in the magical world or had been sent off to Mundania—but that didn't mean the school was unoccupied during those two weeks. All of the school's other denizens remained, with the faculty keeping an eye on the students so everyone behaved themselves, even if class wasn't in session. Would that single two-week period really be long enough for the headmistress to head off to Paris or Rome or someplace equally romantic so she might meet the future father of her unborn child?

Possibly. I thought it would be difficult to cultivate a relationship in such a short amount of time, although I'd be the first to admit that what I knew about the male half of the species was limited at best. I certainly hadn't dated in secondary school, and I had the definite feeling that all of the boys in my area had been warned away from me, since I'd seemed like such a hopeless case. Maybe if I managed to acquit myself well enough here at Miss Primm's, I could look forward to a future that might conceivably include romance.

I shouldn't get ahead of myself, though. I still had most of this year and two more after that to get through before I could declare myself a fully functioning witch, one who might one day have a husband and a family...if I so desired.

Well, eighteen was far too young to be worrying about such things. Even when I graduated from the academy...*if* I graduated from the academy...I still would only be twenty-one, with plenty of time to decide what I wanted from the world. My mother and father hadn't married until they were twenty-six and twenty-eight, respectively, and although my sister Holly was engaged, she was nine years older than I, and again, had had ample time to discover who she was before she'd decided to make such an important decision about her future.

Because Juno was looking at me as I let my thoughts wander, I said quickly, "Maybe that should be our extracurricular activity this year."

"Hooking up with strange men in exotic cities?" she inquired, and everyone laughed, although I noticed the way Helen's cheeks colored…and guessed she wasn't any more experienced about such things than I.

"No," I said severely. "Finding out more about Miss Primm…or all the Miss Primms. There must be some sort of story to discover."

"I doubt the headmistress would appreciate us poking around in her business—" Helen began, but Juno waved a dismissive hand.

"We'll be discreet."

Celeste lifted an eyebrow. We all loved Juno, but "discreet" definitely wasn't a word I would think of to apply to her.

She clearly saw the way we were all staring at her, because she set down her bottle of ginger beer and crossed her arms. Unlike the rest of us, who, while we were wearing jeans, also had on fairly demure button-up tops, she wore a close-fitting knit top splashed in all the colors of the rainbow, with the outline of a unicorn done in metal studs and rhinestones. It was the sort of outfit that had earned her a dubious glance from Professor Hendricks as we passed her in the hall on the way out to our expedition.

Technically, there wasn't a dress code for weekends, when we weren't required to attend classes, but I still thought Juno was probably bending the rules a bit.

"I know how to be discreet," she said, brown eyes challenging.

"I'm sure you do," Celeste replied mildly.

We turned to other topics after that, but it sounded as though we all had a secret project to occupy us during our downtime through the course of that year.

* * *

I HAD TO ADMIT THAT MY LEAST FAVORITE subject was Physical Activities. At least the other courses seemed somewhat relevant to the further development of my magical skills...such as they were...but as far as I could tell, P.A. existed mainly to run us ragged enough that we wouldn't have any spare energy left over to get into mischief.

And what I hated the most about P.A. was team sports.

Not that I minded being on a team with Celeste and Juno and Helen, or the other girls in our year who seemed to have decided they would rather be on our side than otherwise. No, it was that one of the other teams consisted of Mona and Philippa, along with their own particular group of cronies—Eileen Malloy, and Brenda Copperpot, and Sandra Kurtz, all of whom seemed to have decided that this first-year class would be grouped into "us" and "them," for better or worse.

It would have been easy to say that Eileen and Brenda and the rest of them had decided to ally themselves with Mona simply because of her father's position in DOME. However, since my father worked for the same agency and had a position of equal authority, that particular argument didn't hold much water. I honestly didn't see what Mona's appeal could possibly be, but as I'd usually been the odd girl out in my previous school life, my current position didn't seem that strange to me.

And really, I couldn't even say I was on the outside, precisely, since at least now I had a group of friends to rally with and act as my protectors. All the same, even knowing that Juno and the rest of them had my back wasn't enough to reconcile me with the awful fact of being forced to play football against Mona and her gang.

I must confess that I had never been the most coordinated girl in the world. In my previous life, this wasn't too much of an issue, because I carefully avoided team sports and met my P.A. requirements by running or swimming. Such activities weren't an option at Miss Primm's, unfortunately, which was why I spent most of my first autumn there with a lively assortment of bruises on my legs, thanks to contact that was a little too up close and personal during many of the games.

Professor Crenshaw, who oversaw the Physical Activities classes, never seemed to notice that the games got a bit too rough. Perhaps her eyesight wasn't quite what it should have been, or perhaps she thought we all needed some toughening up just in case we failed in our studies here and ended up being sent to Mundania after all.

At least September had already given way to October, and October was now more than halfway over. With any luck, we'd have early snow in November, and that would see the end of our "exploits" on the football field, at least until next spring.

"Not likely," Juno remarked when I stated that hope to her one day after class, and I tilted my head at her.

"Why not?"

She waved a hand. We were trudging back to our room so we could get cleaned up after another bruising match, and—not for the first time—I wondered why PA wasn't scheduled for the end of the day. It seemed silly to get in and out of our gym clothes so we could attend History of Magic afterward.

"This school is run by witches, in case you hadn't noticed," she said. "You don't think they can't snap their fingers and make sure the field is cleared of any snow that might happen to fall?"

I couldn't see myself right then, but I was sure I must have looked quite crestfallen, because Juno chuckled.

"It's not so bad," she said. "I mean, Mona and her little posse are a definite pain, but I think they're just bitter because we keep beating them."

That was true enough. My own clumsiness notwithstanding, we had a pretty efficient team put together. Helen had surprised me by being a fleet-footed and aggressive goalie, and the rest of our group were strong enough players that as long as I stayed out of the way and avoided tripping over my own feet, we managed to do pretty well.

"I suppose that's some comfort," I replied, and Juno grinned.

"Exactly. Now, let's get going, or we're going to be late for history class."

OF US ALL, IT TURNED OUT CELESTE WAS THE most efficient information-gatherer, possibly because so many people were charmed by her accent—she was the only French girl in our class —that those she spoke to often didn't stop to think whether they were passing along tidbits they probably should have kept to themselves. Because of this, we learned that the current headmistress's mother had given birth to her when she was nearly forty, and hadn't actually passed away at all, but had stepped down five years earlier so her daughter could take over.

"Where is the former Miss Primm now?" Helen asked. We'd gathered in the room she shared with Celeste, our homework done for the evening. Technically, there weren't any rules about staying in our assigned rooms after the evening meal was over, and so we often spent this time together. Again, I thought the absence of any strict guidelines was based more on the understanding that those who didn't apply themselves during their time at the academy would end up being zapped to Mundania—or however DOME got those poor unfortunates to that magic-less world. My father would never go into any great detail about the procedure.

Probably for the best.

Celeste gave one of her Gallic shrugs. "No one knows. She addressed the school on the last day of everyone's term and told them it had been an honor to serve as headmistress, but that she knew the academy would be in capable hands with her daughter. And then she disappeared."

A dramatic exit, to be sure. Where would a woman in her seventies go after many decades of service?

Anywhere she wanted, I suppose. Surely the former Miss Primm had earned a comfortable retirement. Or perhaps not; there was no tuition at the academy, as its charter ensured that any students who needed its assistance were allowed entry, no matter what their ability to pay. Did that mean the school had some sort of trust to pay the salaries of its faculty, and our room and board as well?

That seemed to be the most reasonable explanation.

Juno teased out one springy curl and released it. We were all in our pajamas and robes, since we intended to go to bed after our convo. Her robe was bright pink and had llamas wearing sombreros marching across it. Sometimes I wondered how she'd managed to collect so many interesting articles of clothing, but then again, she was from America.

"How old is the current Miss Primm?"

Helen frowned slightly. "That's not a very nice question to ask."

"Oh, for goodness' sake," Juno snapped. "We're not talking about state secrets here."

Celeste watched them both, her expression faintly amused. "I am only guessing, but I believe she cannot be more than thirty-four or thirty-five at the most."

"Then she still has time," Juno replied.

"Time for what?" Helen asked.

"To have a baby, of course," June said. She looked like she wanted to roll her eyes but forbore, for Helen's sake. "Celeste just said her mother had her when she was forty. Maybe that's what all of them have done—waited until they were on top of everything here before having the next Miss Primm."

I suppose that made some sense. Then again, from the few glimpses I'd caught of her, the current headmistress certainly didn't look as though she was planning a romantic getaway to meet the father of her child.

"We'll just have to wait and see," Juno went on. "It makes the most sense that she would go looking for the lucky man during the summer holiday, and that's a long way off."

Too far off, in my opinion. At that point, we had nearly six weeks until Midwinter—a misnomer, I thought, since the holiday actually fell on the solstice and winter's true midpoint was in early February.

And I really didn't want to think about Midwinter. It would be my first real holiday away from my family. I'd told myself that I would do just fine here with my friends…but what if I didn't?

Suddenly, I felt very tired. It had been easy enough to go along from day to day, to take comfort in my minor triumphs and try not to be too discouraged by my inevitable failures. Now, though, I could only think of the long months ahead, and how much work needed to be done during my time here.

Oh, well. I would have to focus on one day at a time…and hope that none of those days would be my last at the academy.

CHAPTER 6
MIDWINTER

Miss Primm stood up at dinner on the fifteenth of December and bestowed a bright smile on all of us in the dining hall. "I have a very special announcement to make!"

She looked happy and glowing, and I experienced a stab of guilt at all the whispering Juno and Helen and Celeste and I had done over the past few months about her personal life. Surely she could have no idea that my little group of friends had spent far too much time speculating as to how she planned to go about achieving the next generation of Primms.

Despite my guilt about our gossiping, I leaned forward in my chair, eager to hear what the head-mistress had to say. Winter had closed in, dark and dank, although there had been very little snow so far...and the small amounts that had fallen were quickly removed from the football field, just as Juno had predicted. Anyway, I was more than ready to hear of anything that might break up the monotony of our days.

Juno also perched on the edge of her chair, brown eyes sparkling. I could tell she was just as ready as I for a change of pace.

"I have spoken with Master Marco at the School for Woeful Wizards," Miss Primm went on. "And we have decided that this year, we will have a joint Midwinter celebration with the students there. Master Marco has graciously invited all of us to his school for a party and dance to be held on the twenty-second."

At once, excited murmurs broke out across the room. Juno put her hands down on the table and gripped the edge, as if that was the only thing preventing her from launching herself upward into a happy dance. My own excitement, however, was immediately tempered by the ominous word "dance" in Miss Primm's announcement. I knew from sad experience that my two left feet on the football field definitely carried over to the dance floor.

Well, I didn't have to dance if I didn't want to. It would be quite enough to get dressed up—I was so glad I'd brought my pretty green velvet dress with me—and to go someplace where there would be new people to meet.

Boys, to be exact. Or perhaps I should have been thinking of them as young men. After all, they were adults between the ages of eighteen and twenty-one, just as the students here at Miss Primm's were as well.

"That is all," she went on. "Enjoy the rest of your meal."

With that said, the headmistress resumed her seat at the high table, and reached for the glass of water at her place setting.

Juno turned to me, eyes glowing. "Please tell me you have a nice dress."

"Of course I have a dress," I returned, somewhat indignant. "Or didn't you notice the velvet gown I've had hanging in the wardrobe the entire time we've been roommates?"

"I don't go poking around in your things," she said primly, and I laughed. "Prim" definitely wasn't a good fit for Juno Hightower.

Being Juno, naturally, she had a party dress. I sometimes found myself shocked at the amount of clothing beyond her school uniforms that she'd brought with her for her stay at the academy. We students were only allowed one suitcase, but she'd managed to cram in enough outfits for nearly a fortnight. If it weren't that I knew her magic was just as unreliable as mine, I would have thought she'd cast a spell on her suitcase to ensure it would carry far more than it had been designed for.

My other classmates weren't quite so lucky. Or rather, following Miss Primm's announcement, a flurry of letters went out to many of the students' families, imploring them to send some party clothes as soon as possible. Technically, while letters could go back and forth, packages weren't allowed—or else care packages filled with everyone's favorite treats would have been arriving daily —but it seemed the headmistress was willing to be lenient in this particular case, since she hadn't given us warning that anything beyond the usual shirts and jeans and jumpers would be needed for extracurricular activities.

Why I'd thought to bring my velvet dress when space in my own suitcase had been at a premium, I wasn't sure. I knew I certainly didn't have the gift of second sight, so it wasn't as if a flash of some hitherto unknown precognitive ability had aided me in making that decision. No, it was probably more likely that I hadn't wanted to leave the dress behind, since it was one of my favorite pieces.

And Mona McGee received such a large box from her parents, Juno was compelled to ask her if she'd been sent an entire new wardrobe.

"Of course not," Mona replied, looking irritated. Whether she was offended by the question itself, or whether she was simply annoyed that Juno had dared to speak to her directly, I wasn't sure. "If you must know, they sent me a coat to match my dress. It's supposed to be quite chilly on Midwinter Eve."

I hadn't thought of that. Naturally, I didn't have anything fancy to put over my party dress. Well, I would just have to make do with my black wool overcoat. At least it was fairly new, since my mother had bought it for me the winter before.

Juno seemed to accept Mona's reply as plausible, because she nodded and said she supposed that made sense. And then the other girl had flounced off, clutching her oversized parcel in both hands.

Classes were conducted all the way up to the day before Midwinter, although none of us were paying too much attention to the lectures, so distracted were we by the upcoming departure from our schedule. In fact, Professor Hamilton lost her patience entirely during Working With Familiars and dismissed us all early, saying it was clear there was no point in trying to make us concentrate when our thoughts were so patently elsewhere.

The unexpected freedom was a gift—but only a limited one, since we still had to attend Physical

Activities and History of Magic afterward. Still, that last afternoon of classes finally wound down, and when the next day dawned, it was with the knowledge that we would be traveling to Master Marco's school that evening to meet the students there.

Bathroom space was at a premium, since everyone was vying for the mirrors there. The four of us had decided earlier there was no point in fighting with the other girls to carve out some room for our prep, and so we'd all congregated in Celeste and Helen's room, since it was a little larger than the one Juno and I shared.

"Your hair is so gorgeous," Helen sighed to me as she watched Celeste set it in long curls, using an enchanted iron her mother had sent all the way from France. "So silky and long!"

I will admit that I was rather vain about my hair, waist-length and flaxen pale. Still, I gave the slightest shake of my head—careful not to disturb Celeste as she was working—and said, "Well, I love your curls—both yours and Juno's."

Juno reached up to touch one of the springy locks she'd let fall around her face. The rest of her hair had been put up and secured in place with jeweled clips, and she looked far older and much more sophisticated than she did when she let it fall free and wild, or had it pulled back in an elastic band. "They can be a pain sometimes," she said. "But honestly, I do like having hair that does its own thing without me having to put much work into it."

"Mine is so frizzy," Helen responded with a sigh.

"It's not frizzy now," I pointed out.

Echoing Juno's gesture, Helen put a hand up to touch her hair. What I'd said was only the truth —Juno had loaned the other girl some of the special serum she used to keep her curls shiny and perfectly formed, and Helen's usually unruly mane now just seemed exotic rather than unkempt.

Honestly, we were all looking quite glamorous that evening. Celeste, of course, never had a hair out of place, and had smoothed her warm brown hair into a complicated twist at the back of her head. Her dress was black, so simple and perfectly cut that she made the rest of us look like we were wearing potato sacks.

All right, that was a bit of hyperbole. My green velvet gown made my blue eyes look almost green as well, and it fit beautifully as well, cut close to the body in the bodice and sleeves, but with an extravagantly full skirt. Juno's dress was shocking violet, with no sleeves and a skirt that stopped above the knee, showing off her long legs. And Helen looked quite elegant in a bright blue sheath with a deep V-neck that revealed cleavage I hadn't even known she possessed.

Celeste had performed her makeup magic on all of us, and I was quite convinced that I probably had never looked better in my life. Even so, I couldn't quite ignore the butterflies in my stomach. Getting dressed up with friends in the safety of one of our rooms was one thing—sallying forth and meeting a bunch of young men for the first time was something else altogether.

Eventually, we were ready, and gathered up our coats and bags so we could head down to the ground floor of the academy. Miss Primm had said that cars would come to fetch us, although she hadn't mentioned where she'd gotten them. As far as I'd been able to tell, the school possessed two official vehicles, one that the cook and the housekeeper used to procure whatever supplies we might need in addition to what was delivered every fortnight, and a big shiny black automobile that appeared to be reserved for the headmistress's use.

The sun had already set, and an icy wind met us as we emerged through the school's front entrance. I was glad of my wool coat, even though it hid the green velvet glory underneath. All around us crowded our classmates, everyone looking very unlike themselves in their elaborate hairstyles and evening makeup.

A long line of vehicles drove up, and we began climbing in. The back seat of each car was big enough to seat four, and so our little group was able to stay together as we were driven away from Miss Primm's academy.

It felt strange to watch the lights of the building disappear behind us, as we hadn't left the grounds since we'd all arrived in early September. But soon enough those lights were gone, and we needed to focus on what lay ahead.

"How far is it, do you think?" Helen asked.

"I don't know," Juno replied. "No one's said anything much about Master Marco's school. But it can't be too far, or taking us there in cars wouldn't be practical. We'd be spending most of the evening driving, which doesn't make much sense."

We all agreed that was true, and settled in to watch the landscape pass by outside the windows. True, because it was dark, there wasn't much to see, but I got an impression of open countryside alternating with forests of some kind, although I couldn't tell what sort of trees grew there.

And then up ahead I saw a warm glow, and realized it was lamp light pouring through a multitude of windows, combined with the flicker of magically powered torches that lined the lane where we drove. As we grew closer, I realized all those windows belonged to an enormous manor house in a style much older than Miss Primm's academy. This place was built of grey stone, and had turrets at either end, although it seemed to me their purpose was more decorative than anything else.

The car slid to a stop in front of the main entrance, which was comprised of two enormous double doors flanked by windows of stained glass. Those doors stood open, allowing a peek inside that showed stone walls and lights everywhere.

We all got out of the car and hurried up the front steps. Since we first-years had been some of the last to be picked up—it seemed the cars had taken us in order of seniority—the place was already lively with the chatter of voices and the sound of music.

If I had come by myself, I knew I probably would have been too timid to push forward into that throng, especially since it was obvious that male voices mingled with the more familiar voices of my classmates. Since I had Celeste and Juno and Helen with me, it was a little easier to pause at the cloakroom so we could all divest ourselves of our coats and then move on to the main hall.

It seemed enormous, much larger than the dining hall at Miss Primm's academy. At one end, a fire roared in a huge stone hearth, while at the other, multiple tables piled with enough food to feed an army immediately drew my attention. We hadn't had any supper, since we were coming to the party, and I was hungry.

"Should we eat first?" I asked, trying not to sound too hopeful.

"Probably," Juno responded, although her eyes were scanning the crowd, as if she wanted to take her measure of the people gathered there before she would allow herself to get distracted. "If nothing else, it'll give us a chance to get the lay of the land."

She headed off toward the refreshment tables, walking confidently in the spiky black shoes she'd put on to complement her brilliant purple dress. How she was able to walk so quickly in heels that high and thin, I had no idea. My own footwear consisted of a pair of delicate black flats—pretty enough, but definitely not the sort of thing that would cause me to trip over myself.

I told myself I needed to act cool, that I couldn't make it too obvious I was trying to get a look around me as I went. The walls held swags of evergreens and red bows, and overhead, enchanted lights shifted and swirled and sparkled, looking like a swarm of multicolored fireflies.

And everywhere there were boys—tall boys and short ones, thin and plump, handsome and plain. Some of them were talking with the students from Miss Primm's—mainly the thirds, as far as I could tell—but many more of them were congregated in uncomfortable clumps, just as the girls from the academy were doing.

Well, I could only hope we would all loosen up as the evening progressed.

There was quite a crush at the refreshment tables, but soon enough, we'd all gotten ourselves plates full of treats—meat pies and sausage rolls and apple tarts and cinnamon-sugar cookies, and so much more that I knew I'd need to circle back for second helpings once I emptied my plate the first time. We headed over to a corner that actually held a few spare chairs no one else had claimed.

"You can sit first," I told Juno magnanimously. "You're wearing the highest heels."

"These things?" she responded with a glance down at the formidable spikes on her feet. "These are nothing."

"They look like torture devices," I said, and Helen giggled, while Celeste only shook her head.

"They are not so bad," she remarked.

The shoes Celeste was wearing weren't quite as high as Juno's, but their heels were just as slender and treacherous. I began to wonder if there were some important matters my mother had left out of my education—namely, how to walk in shoes such as those.

Since there wasn't much I could do about it now, I took a few bites of the food on my plate. Everything was delicious; it seemed the cook at Master Marco's was just as skilled as Miss Greenbriar at my own school.

A moment later, the music stilled, and the crowd parted so I could see all the way to the other end of the hall. Out of the crowd emerged a tall man who appeared somewhat younger than my parents, possibly no more than forty at the most. He had dark hair and eyes, and wore a black frock coat and pants, with a dark red shirt and black cravat.

"Ooh la-la," Juno murmured. "Now, *there's* someone worth looking at."

"He is a bit old for you, don't you think?" Celeste responded, sounding amused.

"I'm just looking," Juno said with a grin. "No law against that, right?"

Celeste only shook her head. "No, I suppose not."

"Good evening, everyone, and welcome," the man said. He had a slight accent—Italian, I thought, even as I realized this must be Master Marco himself. His voice carried clearly to all corners of the room, despite its size, and I wondered if he was using some sort of subtle magic to amplify it so everyone could hear him. "We are very happy to have the students from

Miss Primm's academy here to help us celebrate midwinter—and very happy to have Miss Primm as well."

As he spoke, she stepped forward out of the crowd, and I felt my eyes widen. I'd always thought her very pretty, but that night she looked stunningly beautiful in a long gown of a deep wine shade, setting off her dark hair and eyes. Garnets glinted around the creamy skin of her throat, exposed by the wide neckline of her dress.

"Wow," Juno said. "I've never seen her look like that before."

Neither had anyone else, it seemed, judging by the way the students from her own academy were staring at their headmistress. Actually, a lot of the boys from Master Marco's school were gawking as well, probably wondering if there was any way they could get a transfer so they could have the opportunity to look at that vision every day.

Even Master Marco himself didn't appear unmoved, since his gaze lingered on her for a moment longer than was strictly necessary before he said, "Thank you, Miss Primm, for accepting my invitation."

"No, thank *you*," she responded. Her voice also was clear enough, obviously picked up by whatever amplification spell the headmaster was using. "I'm always pleased to forge new traditions for my students." She turned then and smiled at all the watching crowd. "Enjoy yourselves, everyone—let us have a very happy Midwinter!"

Everyone clapped in response, and then, as she and Master Marco stepped back and the music started up again, they disappeared into the crowd.

For a moment or so, we were all silent. Then Juno said, "Did you *see* how he was looking at her?"

Since I had eyes in my head, of course I had. However, I wasn't sure whether I should start imagining things that might not have even been there.

Helen, on the other hand, didn't seem to possess any such reservations. She let out a sigh and said, "Oh, I can only imagine what it must be like to have a man look at me that way."

"Maybe Miss Primm won't have to look quite so far for the father of the next Miss Primm as we thought," Juno remarked, and Celeste chuckled.

"A man may admire a woman without wishing to be the father of her child," she said. "Still, I will admit that they would make a very handsome couple."

That was true enough. I wondered where they had gone—they were a striking enough pair that I would have thought they'd be easy enough to spot in the crowd, but they seemed to have effectively disappeared. A vanishing spell, possibly...

or maybe something as mundane as Master Marco knowing a convenient exit from the hall in order to steal some private time with the head-mistress.

"Oh!" Helen squeaked next, and we all stared at her.

"What now?" Juno demanded.

Helen's hands were full with the plate she held, so she couldn't exactly point. Just as well, probably, because doing so would have called far too much attention to us. "Don't look now," she said, "but I think a boy is coming over here."

"'A boy'?" Juno echoed. Her gaze slid out toward the crowd in the hall, and she sucked in a breath. "Oh, I think she's right. Six feet of red-haired gorgeousness, heading our way."

It took every ounce of willpower I possessed to prevent myself from staring. As it was, I allowed myself the smallest of sidelong glances, just enough to let me know that Juno appeared to be right. The boy approaching was tall and had red hair—a nice deep russet shade, not the carroty sort of ginger that was often accompanied by far too many freckles. He wore a dark grey suit with a steel-blue vest, and definitely appeared intent on approaching our little group.

He paused a few feet away from us, and seemed focused on inspecting our footwear. Or perhaps he had used up all his reserves of courage in coming over here in the first place, and now didn't quite know what to do with himself.

As usual, Juno came to the rescue. "Juno Hightower," she said, sticking out a hand. "And this is Callie and Helen and Celeste. We're firsts. And you?"

"Lochlan Abernathy," the apparition responded. He had a definite Scottish accent, not so extreme that it was difficult to understand him, but just enough of a burr to make his tenor-shading-into-baritone voice that much more appealing. His gaze slid toward me, and one corner of his mouth lifted slightly in what I thought was an attempt at a smile. "I'm a first, too. You're American, aren't you?"

"Yes," Juno said. "But Callie and Helen, they're Brits, and Celeste is from France."

"Very nice to meet you all," Lochlan said. Once again, his gaze met mine, and an odd little tingle ran down my spine. Still looking at me, he went on, "I was wondering if you might like to dance, Callie."

"Oh, I don't know—" I began, but I didn't get any further than that, since Juno was glaring daggers at me, the sort of look that indicated she would never let me hear the end of it if I didn't take Lochlan up on his invitation. "I mean," I went on hastily, "it sounds like fun—if you don't mind that I'm a terrible dancer."

That hint of a smile he'd been wearing broadened into a grin. "Oh, I'm hopeless, too," he said. "We can do our best not to trip each other. Shall we?"

And he extended a hand to me.

CHAPTER 7

MOONLIGHT MAGIC

Before I could lose my nerve, I reached out and took Lochlan's hand. His fingers were warm and strong and, thankfully, not moist at all. With Juno looking on and smiling—while Celeste appeared amused and Helen just the tiniest bit envious—I let him lead me out to the middle of the floor. It was crowded enough with other dancers that I hoped no one would pay much attention to what the two of us were doing.

Luckily, the music playing was for a slower dance, and so I didn't have to worry too much about performing any wild gyrations. At the same time, it was more than a bit awkward to have Lochlan place one hand around my waist and hold me as we started shuffling around the dance floor together.

The silence began to get too awful, and so I said, "Is this really the first time our two schools have ever shared a Midwinter celebration?"

Lochlan looked infinitely relieved by my question. Clear blue eyes brightening, he said, "Well, I'm a first, like you, so I don't have any personal experience to go on, but it does seem that way. We've noticed that Miss Primm has come and visited here several times over the past few months, and so this must have been what she and Master Marco were planning."

That did seem to be a likely explanation as to why she would have felt compelled to visit Master Marco's school, since even I knew the two institutions each had their own separate courses of study. "I wonder why now," I ventured.

"Absolutely no idea," Lochlan said cheerfully. A pause, and then he added, "Master Marco's only been running the school for the past year, so maybe Miss Primm thought this was a good time to start a new tradition."

Intellectually, I'd known that, but this bit of information still surprised me a little. Unlike Miss Primm's academy, which had been overseen by successive generations of Primms, Master Marco's school was handed off from wizard to wizard, based solely on who was best suited to take over the role of headmaster, a decision rendered by the members of the Council of Magic. Before Master Marco had been Master Magnus, and before him, Master Merrill. Why all their names started with "M"—beyond the obvious alliteration—I wasn't sure. Perhaps it was a prerequisite for the position.

"I think the plan is to have next year's Midwinter party at your school," Lochlan went on.

"Oh, that would be lovely," I said. "The academy is decorated so nicely for the holiday. Not that yours isn't," I added in a rush, not wishing for him to get the wrong impression. "And this hall is very grand, and bigger than ours. But still, I think it's probably a good idea to trade places."

"I'd like to see your school," Lochlan said. His blue eyes—a startling cornflower blue, brighter than mine—still shone down at me, so it appeared I hadn't completely inserted my foot in my mouth. "In fact, I've often wondered why the two schools don't work together more closely. It seems like we're all in this together, so we might as well study together."

I'd wondered that, too. The secondary school I'd attended had been co-ed, so I didn't see why these two institutions for magical misfits couldn't function the same way. Then again, perhaps they didn't want us to be distracted by having all those members of the opposite sex around. The stakes here were much higher than they'd been at my former school.

"Perhaps this is a start," I suggested, and Lochlan nodded.

"Perhaps." A mischievous light danced in his eyes as he asked, "So, how hopeless are you?"

"Horribly," I confessed. "Or at least, I'm *mostly* hopeless. I think I've made a bit of headway these past few months, but it seems like every time I get something right, I get two more things wrong. What about you?"

He grinned, showing the faintest flash of a dimple in one cheek. Oh, yes, he was amazingly good-looking. I still couldn't quite understand why he'd approached me rather than one of my friends, but I certainly wasn't going to complain about my current situation, not when I was out on the dance floor with probably the cutest of the first-year boys as my partner.

"Oh, I'm absolutely pathetic," he said, although he didn't appear terribly dismayed by his status. "I've just finally managed to make the bond with my familiar mostly functional, but I'm an absolute dud when it comes to any real magic."

"Who's your familiar?" I asked, thinking that it might be a good thing to focus on the positive rather than Lochlan's shortcomings as a spell caster.

"He's a raven. His name is Huxley."

Once again, I experienced a stab of familiar envy. "A raven? That sounds fabulous!"

"Yes, he's good to have around. Amazingly smart birds, ravens." Lochlan shuffled abruptly, making me realize he'd been just about to step on my foot before he did that two-step to keep me out of harm's way. Not the most graceful maneuver in the world, but I realized I didn't care much. It was good enough simply to be held in his arms. "What about you?"

"I have a pair of familiars, actually," I replied. Figuring I might as well get the worst over with, I went on, "They're gerbils. Flotsam and Jetsam."

Lochlan didn't even blink. "That sounds like fun. Definitely easier to manage than a raven. Do they ride around in your pockets?"

I chuckled. "Sometimes. Not tonight, of course—this dress doesn't have pockets."

"Yes, I can guess that formalwear and familiars don't usually go together very well."

How was it possible that he could be this nice? I'd never imagined that my first in-depth conversation with a boy my age could go so well, and yet here I was, speaking with Lochlan Abernathy as if we'd known each other all our lives. Possibly our ease stemmed from the simple fact that we were both in the same boat, so to speak, and therefore didn't have much of anything to prove to one another. Still, I found myself wishing this song could go on forever, just so we could keep talking.

That thought had barely entered my mind before the music stopped. I think I managed to prevent myself from frowning in disappointment, but it was a close call.

"Thirsty?" Lochlan asked then. "We can go get some punch, if you like."

Relief rushed through me. It seemed he didn't want our time together to end any more than I did. "That would be super," I replied.

We walked over to the refreshment table. A few feet away, I could see Mona McGee staring at me with what I thought was a mingled glare of envy and dislike. She was actually looking very well, in a simple black dress and a sleek hairstyle which seemed to hint that, while she wasn't a very pretty girl, she might one day grow into her looks and be a handsome enough woman.

No more time to contemplate Miss McGee, however, because Lochlan scooped up two cups of punch and handed one to me, then said, "I know a place we can go where it isn't so crowded."

A nervous little thrill went through me. Was his plan to get me alone so he could take some kind of advantage?

Come to think of it, that might not actually be such a bad thing.

"All right," I said.

The fingers of his free hand slipped into mine, and he led me out of the crowded hall and down a corridor with many doors branching off on either side. We then made our way along another hallway that split off from the first, one ending in a set of double doors that opened onto a balcony.

And not just any balcony, either. It wasn't overly large, but that didn't matter, not when the view before us was so utterly mesmerizing.

Water cascaded over a small waterfall, splashing into the pond below. Dark trees—their branches now bare for the winter—spread their limbs on either side of the stream, while above, a large yellow moon shone down, its reflection glinting in the waters of the pond.

"It's lovely," I breathed. "We don't have anything like this at Miss Primm's."

"I have to say I was impressed when I saw it for the first time." Lochlan lifted his cup of punch to his lips and took a sip, so I thought I might as well do the same. The punch was sweet with fruit juice and had the slightest bit of effervescence, refreshing after our dance. He paused, then said in a much different tone, "I'm glad I met you, Callie Dobkins."

"And I'm glad I met you," I replied, even if "glad" felt like such a flat word to describe the way

I was feeling right then. I knew the punch couldn't be alcoholic, and yet it seemed to bubble through me, making me feel as though I could go floating off into the cold night air. I added, "It will seem like quite a letdown to go back to the academy after this."

He chuckled. "I know how you feel. I suppose we must both hope this event is such a success that Master Marco and Miss Primm will decide to have more get-togethers like it."

"Yes, that's a very good idea," I said, my mind already racing with possibilities. "A picnic on the first day of spring…a dance on May Day…a barbecue at midsummer—"

"All that sounds like a lot of fun," Lochlan responded. "I suppose all we have to do to enjoy those sorts of things is survive the year somehow."

Of course. I'd gotten so caught up in dreaming about ways to divert myself that I'd almost forgotten about our coursework. True, I wasn't failing quite as badly as I'd feared, but I also knew I had a long way to go before I could breathe easy about the whole affair. "Oh, is that all?" I asked airily.

He nodded. Since he was grinning, it didn't look as though he was too worried about the future. Or perhaps he was trying to put on a brave front for a girl he'd just met.

"Yes," he said, "but I'm prepared for the worst.

My magic is definitely subpar, but I've always been very good at maths. I figure I'll make an excellent chartered accountant if I do end up getting shipped off to Mundania."

Lochlan definitely appeared far more sanguine about that particular prospect than I would have been. Since he seemed to be doing his best to keep his tone light, I thought I'd better do the same. "What *is* a chartered accountant, anyway? And how are they different from a regular accountant?"

"I have absolutely no idea," he confessed. "I suppose I'll find out soon enough if I don't come up to snuff."

"Oh, you'll do fine," I told him, even though I didn't know if that was truly the case. "I mean, if someone as hopeless as I am is actually passing their classes, then I would think you don't have much to worry about."

"Here's hoping." Lochlan paused there, then said, "It's probably too soon to kiss you, isn't it?"

I blinked up at him. He was staring down at me, expression earnest, but also diffident, as if he was worried that he'd gone a bit too far with that question.

The logical answer would be that yes, of course it was too soon, since we'd only met each other some fifteen minutes earlier. But it was Midwinter, with a full moon blazing down on us, and the sound of distant music sweet in our ears.

If that wasn't the perfect setting for a kiss, then what was?

"No, it's not too soon," I whispered.

He set his cup of punch down on the stone balustrade and gently plucked the cup from my fingers. Then he bent down and touched his lips to mine.

Even though I'd never been kissed before that moment, I knew the mechanics of how it was supposed to work. I even knew enough to open my mouth to his, to let him taste the punch on my tongue. What I hadn't known was how glorious a sensation it would be, how every inch of my body seemed to become deliciously a-tingle…how I would want it to never end.

Of course it did, just because even the best kiss in the world has to end sometime. He pulled away and straightened up, since he'd had to bend down to initiate the embrace…but he held on to my hands, as if to show he didn't want to put too much distance between us.

"Well," he said, then reached out to touch a strand of my hair. I thrilled at his touch, happy for that small caress. With a smile that seemed to promise everything I'd ever hoped for, he went on, "Let's hope for that picnic on the first day of spring, shall we?"

That question made me understand that he

didn't intend for this to be a one-time thing, that he wanted to see me again.

Could I have been any happier than I was in that moment?

Probably not.

"Yes, let us hope," I said.

I was practically floating on air when I returned to the hall. If my magic had been of any use, I might have been *literally* floating, but as it was, I had to settle for walking alongside Lochlan, still aglow from the last kiss we'd shared before we both decided it was probably a good idea to get back before anyone noticed we'd been gone for a suspiciously long time.

The dance was in full bloom, the floor crowded with students gyrating around each other. My little group had abandoned their corner; I spied Juno spinning enthusiastically around a tall boy with night-black hair and light brown skin, while Celeste was off in a corner talking to an intense-looking young man who appeared as though he might be a year ahead of us, maybe even more. Even shy Helen seemed to have found a companion, a lanky boy a full head taller than she, with hair as blond as mine and thick black glasses.

Clearly, I hadn't been missed. Lochlan and I casually made our way to the refreshment table and helped ourselves to some punch and goodies, then took them over to one side of the hall where we would be out of the way.

"We should write," he said, and I stared up at him.

"'Write'?'" I echoed.

"Write each other," he replied with a grin. "I mean, if we can write home, surely we can write one another as well, can't we? It would be a way to stay in touch until the next event—whatever and whenever that turns out to be."

I could feel my cheeks flushing, and hoped Lochlan would think my heightened color was merely a reaction to the heat of the hall after being out in the cold night air on that balcony. "Of course," I said. "I think that's a wonderful idea."

He appeared pleased that I was willing to go along with the scheme, while inwardly, I allowed myself a happy little twirl at the realization that he wanted to stay in touch with me, that he hadn't taken me out for some moonlight kisses just to keep himself occupied and nothing more.

"Super," he replied. "I'll write first, since I was the one who thought of it."

I agreed that this sounded like a good plan, and for a moment, we stood in silence while we drank our punch and nibbled on bite-size pieces of cake. The song ended, and Juno, who'd apparently spied Lochlan and me standing off to the side, headed over toward us, her dance partner in tow.

"Hey," she said, sounding a bit breathless. I suppose that dancing so wildly in those shoes had been something of a strain even for her. "I was wondering where you two had gotten to. Callie, this is Dev. Dev, this is my roommate Callie."

Her dance partner put out a hand, while Lochlan looked on in amusement. "Well, that's convenient," he said.

"'Convenient'?" I echoed in some mystification.

The lopsided dimple reappeared in Lochlan's cheek. "Dev and I are roommates, just like you and Juno are."

"Well, that's a coincidence," I remarked, but Dev shook his head, mouth twisting in a wry grin.

"Not so much," he said. "I noticed Lochlan dancing with you, and so I thought I'd go over and talk to your friend."

"And the rest is history," Juno put in. "But I think I could use some of that punch, too. Dev?"

She looked up into his face, her big brown eyes inquiring, and he nodded hastily. "Yes, I'm thirsty, too. Nice meeting you, Callie."

"It was nice meeting you," I responded.

The two of them wandered off into the crowd, and Lochlan glanced down at me. "And I say we finish this punch. Ready for another dance?"

"Definitely." Well, actually, I wouldn't have minded sneaking off to our secluded balcony for another round of kisses, but I figured that having another dance with Lochlan wasn't a bad second choice.

I knew I needed to savor as much of the evening as I could, since it wouldn't last forever.

Perhaps not forever, but it was well after midnight when we all bundled ourselves into the waiting cars and were driven back to the academy, with a watchful moon and a panoply of stars overhead. Even though it wasn't a terribly long drive, I still found myself nodding off once or twice, and hoped I'd remain awake long enough to reach our second-floor room.

Everyone else seemed nearly as tired—we weren't used to staying up that late, as it was generally lights out at nine o'clock at Miss Primm's. Still, once we were back inside our room, Juno didn't seem inclined to get ready for bed, other than kicking off her spike-heeled shoes as soon as I shut the door.

"Well?" she said, that one word heavy with significance.

"Well what?" I responded, even though I had a good idea precisely what she was asking.

"You and Lochlan," she replied. "You two disappeared *forever.* What happened?"

"It wasn't forever," I told her. "It was only twenty minutes."

Those deprecating words didn't seem to dissuade her. She plunked down on her bed, oblivious to the way she was wrinkling her party dress. "Twenty minutes is long enough. Dish."

"'Dish'?" I repeated, not sure what she was getting at.

"Spill the tea," she said.

I stared at her blankly.

"Oh, for goodness' sake," she snapped. "Tell me what happened."

As much as I wanted to "spill the tea" on what had gone on between Lochlan and me, I thought it couldn't hurt to leave her hanging for a moment or two. I shrugged before heading over to the closet so I could take off my velvet dress and hang it back up, then climbed into my pajamas. "He took me to a place at the back of the school where there's a lovely balcony overlooking a little waterfall."

"Sounds romantic," Juno agreed. "And?"

"And we talked," I said.

"'Talked'?" she repeated. "That's all?"

"Well...." I drew out the word for a long moment, trying not to giggle at the look of impatience on Juno's face. "He *might* have kissed me."

"I *knew* it!" she exclaimed in tones of some triumph. "You were gone way too long to be doing anything else." A pause, and then she asked, "How was it?"

"Wonderful," I replied, before adding shyly, "It was my first."

She'd been leaning back on her elbows, but that revelation made Juno sit upright and send me a shocked stare. "You made it all the way to eighteen without ever kissing anyone?"

"Well," I said, doing my best not to sound defensive...and probably failing miserably, "I didn't have many opportunities."

"I have a hard time believing that guys weren't lining up to kiss you," she replied. "Most men are suckers for blondes."

I couldn't comment on that generalization. Instead, I said, "Let's just say that the boys where I'm from weren't interested in getting tangled up with a girl who might get shipped off to Mundania at the end of her schooling. It was much easier to have a girlfriend who actually knew how to practice magic."

Juno pursed her lips, then gave a single nod. When she spoke, she sounded much more understanding. "I suppose I can see that. Well, their loss. And besides, not having a boyfriend back home makes you free to see Lochlan Abernathy, so it's all worked out in the end."

I wanted to think so…or at least hope so. "He's going to write to me."

"Very encouraging," she said approvingly. "But we need to figure out a way to get you two together again."

"He told me Master Marco and Miss Primm are thinking about having more of these events," I told her. "So maybe we won't have to wait for too long."

"Perfect!" Juno's smile grew sly, and she added, "I wouldn't be surprised to find out the two of them were also sneaking off for a few moonlit kisses. They were missing for half the evening."

"I didn't see them anywhere," I pointed out, and Juno shrugged.

"That school is a big place. Plenty of places to hide if you don't want to be seen. After all, no one found you and Lochlan, did they?"

I had to agree that they hadn't.

"Anyway," Juno went on, "considering the way Master Marco was staring at Miss Primm, it makes sense that they'd want to come up with a bunch of different ways to spend time together. I suppose now we just have to wait and see what the next party will be…and when."

I'd never been very good about waiting, but I didn't have much of a choice. All I could do was hope that, whatever the headmaster and the headmistress were planning, it wouldn't be too far off in the future.

We were given two days off for Midwinter, blissful days where we went and played in the snow, ate all manner of decadent foods, and spent the rest of our time reading and talking, and then it was back to class. I couldn't help thinking wistfully about the three weeks of winter holiday I'd enjoyed at my previous school, but I told myself this was an entirely different circumstance. All the students at Miss Primm's were expected to pack as much learning as possible into these three short years, and so taking too much time off would be counter-productive.

Lochlan's first letter came just three days after the gala at Master Marco's school. His eagerness only made me that much happier about the connection we'd already forged—even as it made me wish I could be back there with him, talking about our futures, watching the moonlight turn the snowy landscape into a fairyland.

Juno saw the letter, of course—it was difficult to keep much of anything from my roommate—and she pounced immediately.

"Three days, and he's already pining for you," she said. "It must be true love."

Even I knew it was a little early to be bandying that word about. "Don't be silly," I returned, doing my best not to blush. "He said he would write, and he did. There's nothing so terribly extraordinary about that."

"Don't be so sure," she said. "It's not like I got a letter from Dev—or Helen got a letter from Billy, or Celeste got one from Isaac."

"Maybe they're slower writers," I suggested.

"Maybe."

That proved to be the case, because a few days later, all my friends also got notes from the boys they'd met at the dance. What those letters contained—and whether they'd been written because they were all trying to follow Lochlan's lead—I didn't know, but everyone seemed cheerful after that. Lochlan had said that Master Marco was indeed contemplating another party of some sort, and so it seemed as though we wouldn't have to wait too long to see one another again.

This was the sort of news that normally would have put my head in a spin. However, I soon had other matters to distract me, as Professor Hendricks paused in front of the class just a week after Midwinter and intoned, "I have an announcement to make."

All of us looked at one another in thinly veiled dismay. Professor Hendricks wasn't the sort to make announcements, but when she did, they generally were of the kind I didn't want to hear— extra homework, or a surprise quiz where we would be put on the spot and forced to say our answers out loud, much to our collective consternation.

"You have all made good progress so far," she continued. "However, since I believe it's always wise to 'mix things up,' as it were, there will be a competition that takes place now through the end of your term in early August."

A competition? I feared I'd never been the competitive sort, as my poor showing in football could attest. Still, it probably didn't matter whether I possessed that sort of ambitious spirit or not; it appeared I would have to compete now, no matter how much I disliked the notion.

I shifted in my seat, listening to the professor as she continued.

"You will compete in teams of four, so that you can learn to work with one another and assess your individual strengths and weaknesses. At the end of each month, you and your team will be given a task to complete. Points will be awarded for the successful completion of each task. The team with the most points at the end of the term wins."

At once, Juno's hand shot up in the air. Professor Hendricks sent her a look of barely disguised impatience.

"What is it, Miss Hightower?"

"What do we get if we win?" she asked.

The professor blinked at her as if she'd just asked the question in Swahili. "I beg your pardon?"

Undaunted, Juno stared right back at Professor Hendricks. "You said it was a competition. Most competitions have some kind of prize. So, what do the winners get?"

The professor drew herself up to her full height and looked down her long nose at my roommate. "The winners 'get,' as you put it, the satisfaction of a job well done and the pride of knowing that they are well equipped to continue to their second year, Miss Hightower. You are not here for fame and fortune, after all, but to gain the skills necessary to maintain you as a valuable member of our magical world." She paused there, and her gaze moved from Juno to encompass all of us. "I will allow you to choose your own teams. Please have them settled when you return here for class tomorrow morning. That will be all."

She waved a hand, dismissing us, and we all got up from our desks and hurried out. Almost at once, everyone began clumping in little groups, already forming the teams for this "competition."

For us, it was simple enough. Our group was already the perfect quartet, so we didn't see the need to seek out anyone else.

"Although," Juno remarked at lunch later that day, "maybe we aren't going about this scientifically."

"'Scientifically'?" Helen repeated with a blink. "This is magic. What does science have to do with any of it?"

It was true that we didn't have much use for science in our world, not when magic could take care of everything so neatly for us. I'd heard that science ruled Mundania, and so I tended to be wary whenever the subject was mentioned. Still, I was willing to hear what Juno had to say—right then, I thought we needed all the help we could get going into this competition. Was this something new, like the Midwinter ball we'd attended only a few weeks earlier, or was the competition an old tradition that Professor Hendricks had decided to revive, for whatever reason?

Unruffled, Juno reached for an apple and took a large bite. "All I'm saying is that we just naturally decided we'd be on the same team because we're all friends. But maybe it would have made more sense to select our team members based on their various skills instead."

"Or lack thereof," I remarked, with a sideways glance toward the table where Mona McGee sat with her cronies. She seemed remarkably unconcerned about this upcoming competition. Did she know something we didn't?

Juno's mouth quirked slightly. "Yeah, that too. All I'm saying is, it might be better for us to look around a little."

"I don't think that will be necessary," Celeste said. She glanced around at our little group and added, "We have our own combination of skills here. Callie's magic is strong but unpredictable, while I have a very strong bond with my familiar. Your magic, Juno, can be strong as well."

"When it works," she replied with a downward twist of her mouth. Both of us were still struggling with control, although I was doing slightly better in that regard than she.

Celeste shrugged and reached for her glass of water. "Still, it is nothing to discount. And Helen—"

"And Helen is hopeless all around," she cut in, her tone morose.

"That is not what I was about to say," Celeste told her. "I was going to say that your magic isn't very strong, but it's also more reliable. That would be perfect for those situations where timing is important but the strength of a spell isn't."

We all exchanged glances. I had to admit there was something to what Celeste was saying. Individually, we certainly wouldn't light the world on fire, but if we worked on ways to have our magical strengths and weaknesses complement one another, then I thought we might stand a fighting chance.

Juno nodded. "That sounds good. I actually wasn't too thrilled about having to team up with people outside our group, but I was trying to be objective about the situation."

"And now you don't have to," I said. "I just hope Professor Hendricks doesn't throw anything at us that's too dire."

"Oh, she will," Helen said, still not looking very happy about the trials that lay ahead of us.

"But not at first," Juno replied. Unlike our friend, she appeared eager to take on whatever challenges lay ahead. I wasn't quite so keen, but I told myself I'd do my best to survive.

I had to…or face far worse consequences than merely flubbing one of these trials.

* * *

AT LEAST THE COMPETITION WAS SET UP SO each "trial" took place at the end of the month, and therefore we had all of January to get through before we needed to worry about a particular set of tests. Those weeks fairly whizzed by, punctuated by letters from Lochlan and his friends to me and mine, and with growing whispers that there would indeed be a picnic at Miss Primm's academy on the first day of spring, an event to which the young men of Master Marco's school would be invited.

It was good to have that day to look forward to—no need to worry about the weather cooperating, since Miss Primm assured us her magic would make the day a fine one—but it was still many weeks off. In the meantime, we had other things to worry about.

The day of the competition loomed, and none of us had any clear idea of what we were about to face. Professor Hendricks had provided absolutely no clues as to what our first task might be, although Juno assured us it couldn't be anything too terrible.

"After all," she said, as we were gathered in Celeste and Helen's room to plot about what we should do to prepare for the upcoming trial, "it's not as though the professor is going to start us out with something super difficult. She's going to build up to it gradually. I think the most important thing to do is to just stay on our toes and be prepared for anything."

She made it sound so simple, and I hoped she was right. At the same time, I could imagine Professor Hendricks throwing something horrible at the teams right out of the gate so they'd be caught off guard. After all, she was always stressing the importance of maintaining our focus, of not allowing anything to put us off balance in a way that would negatively affect the spells we were casting. A perfect way to test our control would be to hit us with something we hadn't been expecting.

But we could sit here and try to imagine contingencies all night, and it would have absolutely no effect on what the professor was actually planning. That was the problem with magic in the real world, rather than magical theory.

"Good advice," Celeste said. "And I will offer my own. We should go to bed early and get a good night's rest, because being weary and out of sorts will not help any of us."

"True," I said. Even though going to bed would only hasten the next day's arrival, I was tired and cross, and I thought some sleep might help to improve my mood. If I were asleep, I wouldn't be thinking about the upcoming trials.

Unless, of course, they decided to visit my nightmares.

"Okay," Juno replied. "You're probably right about that." She glanced over at me. "Ready?"

I nodded. "I could definitely sleep now."

That seemed to be the end of things, and Juno and I got up from Helen's bed, where we'd been sitting, and headed back to the room we shared. On our way, we passed Mona returning from the bathroom. Her face was shiny and scrubbed; clearly, she'd just gotten done prepping herself for sleep.

"Good luck tomorrow," she said with a saccharine smile, and then kept going before we had a chance to reply.

"What was that about?" Juno asked after we'd reached our room and she'd closed the door behind us.

"I have no idea," I replied, equally mystified. Mona had sent a few especially choice glares in my direction the night of the Midwinter dance after seeing me with Lochlan—and had gone out of her way to avoid talking to any of us since then —so why she'd decided to be magnanimous now and wish us luck in the upcoming trials, I couldn't begin to guess.

However, I doubted it was anything good.

"That girl needs to learn how to relax," Juno said. We were already wearing our pajamas and robes, so all she needed to do was slip off the robe and slide into bed. After she had the covers snugged up to her chin, she added, "I really do think her outlook on life would improve if she'd just let me do her eyebrows."

I laughed. "I doubt she'd ever let you get that close to her face." Once I'd removed my robe and gotten underneath the covers of my own bed, I went on, "I think she's trying to play with our minds, make us wonder about her motivations. It's just another way to get us off balance."

"Lights!" Juno called out, and all the fixtures in the room shut themselves off. Since they were magical by their very nature, they didn't require any of our magic to operate properly. With the room now dark, her next words floated, disembodied, in the darkness. "That does sound like the sort of dirty trick Mona would play. Well, I'm not going to let her get to me. Good night."

"Good night," I echoed, and settled myself against the pillow. My eyes shut, and I breathed in deeply, trying to feel more relaxed than I actually was. Even though I knew Mona was most likely doing her best to play mental tricks on us and that I absolutely should not let her get under my skin, I still couldn't keep my thoughts from racing.

What was she up to...really?

That next morning, I found myself wishing I had any class first thing— even the dreaded Physical Activities— rather than Beginning Spells.

Unfortunately, my wishing wasn't any more effective than my magic.

At breakfast, Helen looked pale and tragic, while Celeste carried on as if absolutely nothing of any real import was going to happen that day. More than once, I'd admired Celeste's *sangfroid;* I had no doubt that even if she didn't manage to get her magic under control and was exiled to Mundania, she'd be running her own company within the year. I still didn't quite know how she managed to be so self-possessed and yet so hapless with magic at the same time, but I wished I could borrow some confidence from her.

I wasn't very hungry, but I made myself eat anyway, since I knew that facing any kind of ordeal on an empty stomach was never a good idea. Juno ate with what appeared to be good appetite, although Helen picked at her food and left half of it on her plate. Celeste had her customary half a grapefruit and an egg white and feta cheese omelet, and appeared to carry on just as she did every other day.

Failure doesn't mean you're going to be expelled or shipped off to Mundania, I reminded myself as we all trooped out of the dining hall and down the corridor to Professor Hendricks' classroom. *It just means you won't earn any points. Surely that isn't the end of the world, is it?*

All those facts appeared to be true. On the other hand, I didn't precisely know what earning points even meant, except to prove you were better at controlling your magic than your fellow classmates. Still, while I wanted to make a good showing, I also needed to remember that failure in one task didn't mean failure in all of them. I would have six more chances after this one to prove my ability.

Such as it was. While I'd so far managed to avoid blowing up a classroom or turning my two gerbils into a pair of carousel horses, I hadn't exactly lit the world on fire, either.

You don't need to set the world on fire, I told

myself. *You just have to survive your time here so you can get on with your life.*

It was something of a relief to enter the classroom and see that everyone assembled there looked just as worried as I, even Mona's faithful shadow, Philippa Carmody. The only person who didn't appear to have a care in the world was Mona herself. She sat at her desk, idly playing with one lock of inky black hair as she wound it around her finger, and she even wore a faint smile.

What was going on there? Had she been doing the same thing as I—namely, continually reassuring herself that her performance in this one task wouldn't determine her future at the school, and so she had no reason to do anything but relax?

If that was what was currently going on in her head, then she was doing a better job of calming herself down than I. My reflection in the mirror that morning had looked pinched and tired, even though I'd gotten a little more than eight hours of sleep. Clearly, all my inner reassurances weren't doing much to help me.

The murmurs of the students died down as Professor Hendricks swept into the room. She didn't look any different—in fact, she wore the same severe black skirt suit that she'd had on for my first day of class—and yet I fancied there was still something not quite the same with her, something I couldn't quite put my finger on. Was it only that she carried an extra aura of anticipation around her this morning, a desire to know how her students were going to acquit themselves in this first trial?

Possibly. I folded my hands on my desk and drew in a deep breath, and reminded myself that at least I wasn't doing this alone, that I had my friends to help get me through the experience.

"Good morning, class," Professor Hendricks said formally. "The day of the first challenge is here. The task is a simple enough one—you will need to recite a charm that creates an echo of your voice so you can throw it anywhere you like."

As usual, Juno's hand was the first in the air. I didn't think her eagerness was so much a desire to be a star pupil, and more that she wanted to be the first to get any necessary clarifications out of the way.

Just the mildest resignation tempered Professor Hendricks' tone. "Yes, Miss Hightower?"

"What do you mean, 'throw your voice'?"

"Like this," the professor replied…only the sound of those words didn't appear to be emanating from her throat, but rather from a corner of the room directly behind us. "It's a very simple spell, and one that doesn't leave much margin for getting out of hand. So to speak," she added, with a significant glance in my direction.

I had a feeling I would never live down the incident of the attacking vines. So far, it had been the most spectacular backfire of our first-year class.

"You have five minutes to decide who in your groups will cast the spell," she went on. "After that, we will have the teams participate in alphabetical order."

Since we'd made Celeste Saint-Michel the nominal captain of our team, that meant we would go last. I found myself wondering whether I should have taken on that role—but no, probably better to let the other teams go first so we could see how they acquitted themselves and alter our strategy as needed.

Whatever that strategy turned out to be.

All the teams went into their various huddles. Helen was biting her lip, a sure sign she didn't think she was up to the task ahead.

"I have no idea how a spell like that is even supposed to *work,*" she moaned.

"It's all right," Celeste replied, unflappable as ever. "I think all I need to do is cast a ventriloquism spell."

"You know how to do that?" Juno asked. From the way her brows drew together, it looked as though she wasn't entirely sure our friend even had such a spell in her arsenal.

"In theory," Celeste said.

That didn't sound very promising. "'In theory,'" I repeated, my tone flat.

"Yes," she said. "I've spent a lot of time reading spell books, looking up things we haven't covered yet in class. In *theory*"—she added extra emphasis to the word, mouth pursing a bit as she met my gaze—"it would be no different from casting any other spell. As they've been teaching us for months, the most important things are focus, concentration, and intent. For others, magic comes easily, and they don't have to put so much effort into it. We are not so lucky—but that doesn't mean we can't be successful on our own terms."

She sounded so sure of herself. I had to hope she was right; while what she had said was true enough, I knew that sometimes these things didn't go so smoothly when put to the test in the real world.

But I knew we needed to let Celeste try. Maybe all of us should have been reading spell books and doing our best to expand our knowledge of the magical arts, but honestly, I had a hard enough time keeping up with the regular coursework that I didn't know where I'd find the time for extracurricular activities such as those.

"One minute to go," Professor Hendricks intoned, and Juno let out a breath.

"All right," she said. "Celeste goes to bat for us on this one."

She didn't add, *I hope you know what you're doing,* but the dubious expression my friend wore seemed to indicate she wasn't sure this wouldn't all end in tears.

I certainly hoped not. Then again, the professor had obviously started us off with a fairly innocuous spell to mitigate the chances of anything too horrible happening if something went awry.

"It's time," Professor Hendricks said. "Team one?"

Abigail Andrews stepped forward. She was a tall girl with hair nearly as fair as mine, and always made me think of a Valkyrie, since she was broad-shouldered and athletic as well. Today, however, she looked less like someone who would be fighting side by side with her Viking kin and more like a girl who very much wanted to find a hole and crawl into it.

"Ready, professor," she said, although she didn't sound very ready.

Apparently, Professor Hendricks had already decided it was best to ignore any outward signs of nervousness, because she said briskly, "Very good, Miss Andrews. Please, go ahead and perform the spell."

Alice's fingers twisted in her tartan skirt. Her

lips moved, but I couldn't hear what she was saying. In fact, her eyes widened in horror and surprise as she opened her mouth to speak…and nothing came out. One of the other girls in her group—Misty Cantu—stepped forward and also tried to say something, but only ended up mouthing words none of us could hear.

"Ah," said Professor Hendricks after an uncomfortable pause. "I think I see the problem. Audio!"

As soon as those syllables left the professor's lips, Misty and Alice both started talking at once.

"Why couldn't I hear anything?"

"You did it wrong—I knew you would!"

"Girls," the professor broke in, holding up a hand. "Yes, it seems that Alice's spell backfired, and canceled her voice entirely rather than throwing it as instructed. And the spell's area of effect caught you, Misty, which is why you couldn't speak, either. But at least that shows your magic was working, Alice, even if it didn't create the desired outcome. Remember to maintain your focus always—and better luck next month."

Looking dejected, the two girls sat down by the others on their team, both of whom appeared extremely annoyed. While I understood their disappointment, at least they could be safe in the knowledge that Alice's misfire hadn't caused any permanent damage.

Two more teams made their attempt after that. Susan Davenport did manage to throw her voice—sort of—but it was so quiet that it mostly sounded like a hiss coming out of a far corner of the room, rather than the sort of hearty declaration Professor Hendricks had wanted. And Louise Langford's voice came out of her throat in such a bellow that the professor had to stop the spell immediately so it wouldn't deafen the lot of us.

And then Mona McGee stepped up. I suppose I shouldn't have been surprised that her team would have made her its captain; she was the sort who had to be in charge no matter what she did. However, I didn't know whether doing so was such a good strategy, considering she had yet to pull off a successful spell. If I had to guess at their reasoning, however, I would have conjectured that her teammates simply hadn't wanted to get in an argument with her over the subject.

Her mouth opened, and immediately from a far corner of the classroom came the words, "Is this how it's supposed to work?"

Professor Hendricks' eyes widened in surprise before she apparently realized that she was supposed to maintain a neutral expression. Immediately, her face went still, but she said in approving tones, "Excellent, Miss McGee. Flawless execution. You may sit down."

Mona nodded, and a smile of triumph spread

across her lips—a smile that belied the demure-ness of her voice as she replied, "Thank you, Professor Hendricks."

She went to rejoin her teammates, and the professor said, "Celeste Saint-Michel?"

Cool as ever, Celeste got to her feet. Juno and I exchanged a worried glance. As Professor Hendricks had said, Mona's performance was pretty much flawless. Even if Celeste was able to pull this off—and as much as I hoped she would, I didn't know whether she could—she would have to do an even better job than Mona had.

Like the other girls, Celeste opened her mouth to speak. Unlike the others, what emerged from her lips was Professor Hendricks' dry, brisk tones.

"But I know I thought the words of the spell correctly!"

"Clearly, you missed something," the professor returned…only in Celeste's lilting French accent.

"Oh, no," I moaned, sounding very American.

"You took my voice!" Juno exclaimed…except that was my proper English intonation instead.

Everyone started talking at once—in voices that weren't their own. Over the pandemonium, Professor Hendricks called out, still sounding very French, "Girls, please! I can fix this."

Her mouth moved…saying the words of a counter-spell, I assumed. Celeste stammered, "I—I still do not understand—"

And, thank goodness, she sounded like herself once more. Everyone began speaking again, except this time, to reassure themselves that they had their own voices back and no longer sounded like one of their compatriots.

"Well," the professor said. A small pause as she looked over at Celeste, who had gone silent and resumed her seat, obviously realizing this was not the time for further protests. "That was an interesting exercise. I think it clearly showed the various ways in which a spell can go wrong. Luckily, there was no lasting damage—but I think we all know now how important it is to focus before embarking on any spellwork, no matter how trifling it might seem." She went silent again, and then offered Mona a smile. "Miss McGee, you and your team have won this month's contest. Congratulations."

The girls on Mona's team all grinned at each other, although I noted she was still able to take a moment to offer me a spiteful glance. I lifted my chin and looked away, even as I tried to tell myself that this was only the first contest and we would have plenty of opportunities to redeem ourselves in the coming months.

Even so, the loss stung.

* * *

Supper that night was uncharacteristically subdued. True, Mona and her cohorts were still gleeful about their victory, but the rest of us in the first-year class had very little to be happy about.

Juno pushed some mashed potatoes around on her plate and said, "You should have let me cast the spell."

"Oh, and you would have done so much better?" Celeste retorted. She set down her fork and reached for the glass of water next to her plate. "You barely study."

"Sometimes it's not about studying," Juno shot back. "It's about natural talent."

"I haven't seen so much evidence of that, either."

Juno bristled, and I pulled in a breath, realizing I needed to play peacemaker before the situation got too out of hand.

"It was just one contest," I said quickly. "There'll be others. Fighting about it isn't going to change anything."

Both girls settled against their seats, looking shamefaced.

"I am sorry," Celeste said. "It is only that we have been sitting here, trying to eat, and Mona keeps looking over at us and laughing."

Helen pursed her lips. "She's doing that to

everyone, actually. At least she's an equal-opportu-
nity mocker."

That much was true. She might have bestowed
a few more of those gloating glances on our little
group than on some of the other teams, but no
one had escaped unscathed.

"This isn't about Mona, anyway," I said. "Yes,
she managed to win this month's contest. That
doesn't mean she'll win any of the others."

This comment got nods from the rest of the
group, even as I wondered how my nemesis had
managed to pull off such a feat. We'd spent five
months here at Miss Primm's academy already, and
this was the first time I'd seen even a flicker of talent
from Mona McGee. It wasn't even that she'd experienced spectacular failures, like my attacking vines or
Celeste's ventriloquism spell gone wrong, or the time
Abigail Andrews had tried to magically fill a vase with
water and instead had made the ceiling rain, soaking
all of us almost instantly. No, it was more that whenever Mona attempted a spell, absolutely nothing
happened at all. One would have thought she was
surely destined for a new life in Mundania, and yet
she had certainly succeeded spectacularly today.

Well, perhaps it was only that the very tiny bit
of magic she possessed worked in very specific
instances, and she had gotten lucky in terms of
the particular magical test Professor Hendricks

had devised. I couldn't really think of any other plausible explanation.

"We have to make sure she doesn't win any more trials," Juno said, and the dejected expressions Helen and Celeste had been wearing were replaced by ones of determination.

Yes, that was better. Mona and her team might have beaten us once, but that didn't mean it would happen again.

UNFORTUNATELY, THE TEST AT THE END OF February saw Mona and her friends once again claiming victory. This time, the trial involved conjuring an image and projecting it on one of the walls. She put up a picture of a beautiful seaside town, possibly in Greece, and held it there for several minutes. We had decided Juno would be the one to attempt this task, since she tended to do better with enchantments that involved illusions than the rest of us.

However, the picture she tried to project—of a herd of galloping horses—turned into the real thing, as we were all forced to scatter when a number of the enormous beasts leapt off the wall and tore through the classroom, knocking desks over and sending girls flying before Professor Hendricks recovered herself enough to utter the words of the counter-spell, sending the horses back whence they came—and forcing the rest of us to spend the remainder of our class time putting the furniture back in order.

But once again I tried my best to console my friends, reminding them we still had months to go, and besides, the rest of the girls in our class were in the same boat. It could have been worse.

I knew some of my sunny outlook on the situation had to do with the rapid approach of the first day of spring, and also the picnic planned with the students from Master Marco's school. It was hard to be too glum with the prospect of that outing coming in the next several weeks.

And sure enough, the auspicious day dawned bright and sunny, promising to be warmer than normal. If Miss Primm had invited casual conversation, I might have asked her if she truly had cast a spell to ensure the day would be fine, since she'd hinted earlier that she had such a plan up her sleeve in the case of inclement weather. As it was, I only sent a silent thank-you winging out into the universe that we had sun rather than rain, and that we wouldn't have to bundle up in coats and scarves while having our picnic.

Because the event was being held on the grounds of the academy, we had little to do to get ready except put on outfits suitable for the day and wait for the long line of cars bringing the students from Master Marco's school. Sure enough, they arrived promptly at eleven-thirty, and disgorged all the young men we'd been so eagerly awaiting.

Lochlan's bright, coppery hair was easy to pick out from the crowd, and I lifted a hand to wave him over. Next to him were Dev and Billy and Isaac, who also brightened as they saw my friends standing next to me.

"There's a big pavilion out back where we can load up our picnic baskets," I said as soon as they came close enough to hear me. As much as I would have liked to give Lochlan a hug, I thought it was probably better to refrain from public displays of affection while we were surrounded by such a crowd.

"Sounds great," Lochlan replied. His eyes were dancing, telling me he had guessed exactly why I was being so circumspect.

"Definitely," Dev put in. "I'm starving."

"Hi, Dev," Juno commented. "Nice to see you."

He grinned, teeth flashing white against his brown skin, and leaned in to give her a quick kiss on the cheek. "Nothing against you, Juno," he said. "But a growing boy needs to keep his energy up."

"Then we'll have to do something about that," she replied. "Come on."

Our little group headed toward the back of the school, where a large white pavilion had been erected for the event. We weren't the only ones with food uppermost in their minds, apparently, because almost everyone was going in the same direction. In fact, I noted Mona McGee a ways off, a gangly boy with unruly sandy hair at her side. I couldn't recall seeing her with anyone at the Midwinter dance, but since Lochlan had occupied me for a large portion of the evening, I suppose that wasn't so strange.

But soon enough Mona slipped from my thoughts, because it was time to grab picnic baskets from the table where they'd been supplied, and to load them up with sandwiches and fruit and cheese and wonderful little fruit pies small enough to fit in the palms of our hands. Soon enough, our group had wandered off into a small copse that offered plenty of fallen logs where we could perch and feast on the food Miss Primm— or, more accurately, Miss Greenbriar—had provided.

I hadn't seen either the headmistress or Master Marco, but then, we'd been one of the first groups to head off into the countryside, so I didn't think much of it. For a few moments, we were busy divvying up the food and pouring out ginger beer or water from the bottles we'd brought along.

Then Lochlan said, "How's the term going for everyone?"

Juno made a face, and the rest of us burst out laughing.

"That good?" Isaac inquired before taking a bite of his sandwich. He and Celeste had gotten comfy on a log only a few feet away from the one where Lochlan and I sat; there were four such logs arranged to make a rough square, and I guessed that someone else had used this little clearing as a picnic spot in the past.

"We're hanging on," I said. "But so far, Mona McGee's team is beating everyone in the monthly competitions, and none of us are too thrilled about that."

Lochlan tilted his head. "Do they matter so much, these competitions?"

"You don't have them at your school?" I asked, surprised.

"No," he said. "Maybe the professors thought a fight might break out over them—we boys fancy a scrum more than you girls, I should imagine."

Possibly. My brother Jacob and his friends had roughhoused much more than we girls ever did, and I could see how the boys at Master Marco's school might allow the competition to get physical if they were frustrated enough by the results.

I nodded, and Celeste said, "The trials aren't a prerequisite to moving on to the next year or anything like that. It's only that winning earns everyone on the team extra points, and those can sometimes make the difference if someone's scores in their other classes are right on the edge."

Our male companions absorbed this information, with Lochlan saying, "Then it's nothing much to worry about, is it? I mean, it's great if you win, but not winning isn't going to hold you back."

"Unless we flunk all our finals," I responded, my stomach knotting despite my desire to focus only on this glorious spring day, and the very welcome feeling of having Lochlan sitting right there next to me.

"You won't flunk," he said, clearly trying to cheer me up. "I've gotten all those letters from you, remember? You're a very clever girl."

Perhaps I was. I'd always done well in the nonmagical subjects—language and maths and geography. But knowing that Ankara was the capital of Turkey wasn't going to do me a bit of good when it came to corralling my unruly magic once finals came around in August.

"Yes, she is clever," Juno said stoutly. "We all are. And that's why I'm declaring a moratorium on talk about school. It's too nice a day for that."

"Amen," Helen intoned, and we all laughed.

After that, the discussion moved on to the other intramural outings that had cropped up on the schedule—a May Day bonfire, another dance at Midsummer. By the time we'd exhausted those topics, we'd made a sizable dent in the food in our picnic baskets, and by tacit agreement, broke up into couples so we could all get some alone time with our respective significant others.

Lochlan took me by the hand and led me away from the little woods where we'd had our picnic, and off to a spot where a small stream cut through newly green grass. The only sounds were the rustle of the wind and the song of a lark somewhere off across the meadow.

"Better," he said.

"You don't like my friends?" I asked, knowing that probably wasn't what he'd meant.

"I like them very much," he replied. "Just not as much as I like you."

I tilted my head, trying my best to look innocent. "Well, I suppose that's only natural."

He chuckled, then bent down and kissed me, his mouth sweet with ginger beer and apple pie. It felt amazing to stand there in the sun and feel his arms around me, for in a moment like that, all my concerns about school and competitions and tests seemed very far away.

When we pulled apart, I said, "I wish we could see each other more often."

"I know," he replied. "But I suppose we

should simply be glad that the Midwinter ball wasn't a one-off sort of thing."

True. I still didn't quite understand their motivations, but it seemed that Miss Primm and Master Marco were giving the students at their respective schools more opportunities to spend time with their counterparts than any previous classes had been provided, so I supposed that we needed to count our blessings.

"Yes, that's fair enough," I replied. "Only—"

"Only what?"

I hadn't said anything to him in my letters about the upcoming occasion, because I hadn't wanted him to think he was obligated to do something special for me. Still….

"Only it's my birthday next week," I said, "and I wish I could see you then, too."

At once, Lochlan reached out and took my hands. "Why didn't you tell me it was going to be your birthday? I would have brought something for you."

"That's precisely why I didn't tell you," I said. "I didn't want you to feel obligated to get me anything."

And actually, it probably would have required him to ask his mother to shop for a birthday present, since it wasn't as though he could have gone out and selected something for me himself. Like the girls at Miss Primm's, the boys at Master

Marco's school were very locked down. Except for outings such as this picnic, they were just as trapped as the rest of us.

"Still—"

I went on my tiptoes and pressed a quick kiss against his lips to get him to stop talking. A little surprised by my own boldness, I said, "All I really want is to spend time with you. It would have been nice to do it on my birthday itself, but since it's less than a week away, this is the next best thing."

"Tell you what," he said, locking his hands with mine, "we'll have a real blowout for you once we've both graduated and can do what we like. Does that sound like a plan?"

I nodded, even though I wasn't sure how hopeful I could be about such a dubious future. "But what if we don't graduate?"

That morose question earned me a chuckle. "We will, Callie." Lochlan's blue eyes locked on mine, practically willing me to believe what he was saying.

"You sound very positive," I told him, and his shoulders lifted.

"I have to be. That's what's getting me through all this." He let go of my hands so he could run his fingers through his hair, pushing back the lock that always threatened to fall over his forehead. In the sunlight, that hair burned like copper fire. I wanted to reach out and touch it, but I held back, not sure whether I should take that kind of liberty. "Even if the worst happens—"

"We both fail, and get sent to Mundania?"

His jaw tightened a bit, but his tone was casual as he said, "Yes. Even if that happens, I'll find you. I don't know how, but we can be together, too, if we believe hard enough. I can be a chartered accountant, and you—"

He stopped there, as if he wasn't quite sure of an occupation mundane enough to match being a chartered accountant.

"And I can be an advertising executive," I offered. I only had the very vaguest idea as to what an executive did, let alone one who worked in advertising, but it did sound as though it must be rather tedious.

"Yes, that," Lochlan said with a grin. "But honestly, I don't think we'll be forced to such extremities."

"You really don't?" Because although I wasn't sure I could be quite as hopeful as he, I wanted his reassurance that everything would work out in the end.

He took my hand again, his fingers closing around mine, warm and comforting. "I really don't," he said. "Look at it this way—if we hadn't both been sent to these schools, we probably would never have met each other. That tells me we already have the universe on our side. Everything else is just distractions."

"'Just distractions,'" I echoed, and he flashed me a sunny smile that made me feel warm all over.

"Precisely."

He bent and kissed me then, and I let myself melt into his embrace.

It was good to be distracted sometimes.

CHAPTER 10

GOING TO SEED

Although I couldn't have Lochlan with me on my birthday, I could have my friends, and that was almost as good. Juno coaxed Miss Greenbriar to bake me a gooey chocolate cake, and the four of us sat in Helen and Celeste's room and laughed and talked and ate far too much.

"I'll bet you're counting the days until May Day," Juno teased me.

"Thirty-eight," I said, after licking some chocolate frosting off my fork. "Why do you ask?"

She grinned rather than reply, and Helen said, "Well, I'm keeping track, too. I can't wait to see Billy again!"

"Oh, so you're getting serious also?" Juno asked. "Maybe you and Callie can have a double wedding."

Helen's cheeks flushed pink, and mine heated as well. Trying to sound severe—and failing horribly—I said, "I think it's a bit premature to be talking about weddings when we've only seen the boys twice."

"And because you're both only eighteen, and need to finish your coursework before you can even think about such things," Celeste put in.

"Nineteen," I corrected her. "I'm the old woman here."

Because I, with my late March birthday, was the oldest of our little quartet. Juno's birthday was at the end of July, and Celeste and Helen were both in September, although at opposite ends of the month. Being nineteen didn't feel much different from being eighteen, however, and I wondered if that would change when I turned twenty a year from now and finally left my teens behind.

"Close enough," Juno said, and reached for the knife so she could cut herself a second piece of cake. I didn't object, even though I was still on my first slice. There was plenty to go 'round, after all.

And though I missed my family, and had allowed myself a few wistful thoughts about what my birthday might have been like if I'd still been at home, I couldn't allow myself to get too melancholy. I had friends here, and even if I wished I could have seen Lochlan on my special day, I

remembered that I would see him soon enough…
in thirty-eight days, to be precise.

We had two more trials to get through before
then, unfortunately.

ONCE AGAIN, MONA'S TEAM TOOK THE PRIZE
in the competition at the end of March. The task
then was to make music appear out of thin air.
Somehow, she managed to make it sound as
though an entire symphony orchestra was playing
in the room with us. Our little team did better
than I'd thought, since Helen surprised everyone
on our team by conjuring the sounds of a single
melancholy guitar, but one guitar wasn't enough
to beat an entire orchestra, unfortunately, and
there weren't any points for second place.

But as the weather warmed up and we were
able to spend more and more time out of doors
when we weren't studying, our spirits lifted despite
our string of defeats. At least, as Juno continued
to point out, all the other girls in the first-year
class were doing just as poorly as we were, and so
we couldn't exactly claim to be in last place.

"And I know we'll do well in the April competition," she said, curls bouncing in enthusiasm as
she waved a hand. Professor Hendricks had
announced the theme the day before, and Juno

had immediately seized on the opportunity. "Callie, you're better with your familiars than anyone in the class."

Because that, it seemed, was going to be our next challenge. The professor had told us it would have something to do with working with familiars, although she hadn't gone into any particular details.

And Juno was right—or at least partially right. Working With Familiars was definitely my best class, although some might have said that was damning with faint praise. Besides, Celeste also worked very well with her Siamese cat Mignon, even if that feline specimen always acted as though she was bestowing favors rather than carrying out her mistress's commands.

However, Mona McGee was absolutely horrible at getting her white rat to do anything at all, and so it seemed as though this time I might actually have a chance at beating her.

Admitting such a thing, however, only seemed like an open invitation to the universe to have something go terribly wrong, and so I said, "I don't know—Philippa does pretty well with her squirrel. And Abigail's little dog is awfully smart."

That was no exaggeration—what her tiny little teacup Chihuahua lacked in size, he made up in brainpower, and he had a very close bond with Abigail Andrews. My connection with Flo and

Sam had grown by leaps and bounds during the time I'd been at the academy, and yet I still wasn't sure whether it would be enough to win the day.

"And your gerbils are very fast and do everything you tell them to," Juno replied. "It's going to be great."

I thought her remark was a bit overblown. The little creatures had more of a spirit of competition than I'd expected, and I got the definite feeling that they wanted to put on a good show so they'd look good compared to all the other familiars, and yet I still didn't know whether that would be sufficient for us to finally score a win.

Well, I'd find out soon enough.

With three of these trials already under my belt, I didn't feel quite so anxious as I walked into Professor Hendricks' classroom the next morning. Still, this was the first time my team had put all their faith in me, and I fervently hoped I wouldn't disappoint them.

I did feel a bit better to see that Mona was looking pale and pinched, and not nearly as confident as she'd been during the previous three trials. Her teammates also didn't appear terribly assured, either, which seemed like a good sign.

But Abigail sailed in like she was ready to conquer the world, her Chihuahua Adolphus riding in her book bag, and I swallowed. The dog's little black eyes were fixed on me, as if he knew I was the only one he needed to worry about.

Or rather, the two little creatures currently hiding in my pockets. Flo poked out her head to look around the room—and possibly assess the competition—but Sam stayed safely ensconced inside his pocket, clearly not wanting to emerge until it was necessary.

We all took our favorite seats, and Professor Hendricks entered the classroom. To everyone's surprise, she had a large robin perched on her shoulder, its rusty red breast a bright splash against the professor's severe dark suit. "This is Boudicca," she told the assembled students as she took her usual place at the lectern. "In general, I try not to bring her to class, since I don't want there to be any distractions, but she's going to help me assess your familiars' performance today." A nod toward the bird, and she flew off her shoulder and took a perch on the chair behind the desk—a chair the professor rarely used. Once there, the robin ruffled her feathers a bit and appeared to survey the classroom, as though taking our measure one by one.

"Now, then," Professor Hendricks went on. "This is a test that will measure your ability to communicate with your familiars, and also to track how well they follow your orders." She went to her desk, opened a drawer, and drew out a large muslin sack. Without speaking, she untied the bit of string that held one end closed and then upended its contents onto the floor in front of the desk.

A bewildering mixture of seeds poured out of the sack, everything from large striped sunflower seeds to tiny little grains of millet, barely visible against the warm-toned oak floor. A low gasp made its way around the room as those of us watching began to get an idea of what the professor had planned.

"You will instruct your familiars to bring you one of each kind of seed and deposit it on your desk. This means you will need one millet seed, one flax seed, one grain of wheat, one grain of rice, one poppy seed, and one sesame seed. Points will be deducted for missing seeds, or two of the same kind instead of one of each. You will have five minutes for your familiars to complete the task."

Next to me, Juno frowned, her fingers nervously stroking the brilliant plumage on Fred's back. Celeste and Helen also looked worried, although neither of them said anything. They knew this was one trial I would have to manage on my own.

I reached in my pockets and pulled out Flo and Sam. They crawled up my arms, their tiny claws digging into the heavy knit of my uniform cardigan.

"Professor Hendricks!" Mona called out. She was staring at me, eyes narrowed, and my stomach made an uneasy flip-flop.

"Yes, Miss McGee?"

"I don't think it's fair that Callie has two familiars. She'll be able to get the task done in half the time."

Ugh. I hadn't even thought of that angle, but leave it to Mona to find any possible weakness and try to take advantage of it.

Professor Hendricks tilted her head to one side. "I see your point—"

My stomach clenched further.

"—but on the other hand, she will have to expend the mental energy to work with two familiars at once, which is more difficult than controlling only one. I think it will all come out even in the end. But thank you for your concern."

That last comment made it clear that Professor Hendricks wasn't going to limit me to working with only one gerbil. I couldn't quite let out a sigh of relief, but I also felt just a little less nauseated.

"Any other questions?" she asked.

Everyone remained uneasily silent. The professor gave us a thin smile.

"Very good." She paused, and picked up the

silver pocket watch which hung from the chate-
laine at her waist. "Then…the trial starts now."

I gulped in a breath of air and patted Flo and
Sam's tiny little heads. They were warm and reas-
suringly soft, but that wasn't why I touched them.
For whatever reason, it was often easier for me to
communicate with my familiars when we were in
direct contact.

See the grain? I told them. *See all the different
little bits? You need to run over there and get me
one of each kind, and bring it back and put it on
my desk.*

They both tilted their heads at me, as if trying
to figure out why I would ask them to do something so silly.

It's all right, I assured them. *Just go and get
the seeds.*

Their noses wriggled, and then they scampered down my sleeves, hopped on my desk, and
leapt onto the floor. I suppose that would have
been a terrible drop for an ordinary gerbil, but
familiars possessed physical abilities far beyond
what their "normal" counterparts might have been
able to manage.

All around me, my classmates had their familiars performing similar tasks. Or rather, it seemed
they'd communicated with them silently much the
way I'd spoken to Flo and Sam, but, unlike my
gerbils, their familiars weren't moving post-haste

to the front of the room where the seeds lay. Philippa's squirrel—it appeared Mona had realized there was no way in the world she could get her rat familiar to behave himself—had begun to run toward Professor Hendricks' desk but then had stopped part of the way there, tail flicking about wildly as if it wasn't quite sure what it needed to do.

Abigail's Chihuahua sat shivering in her arms, clearly unwilling to get down. My classmate let out an impatient hiss from between her teeth and bent over so she could set the dog on the floor. For a moment, he stood next to her desk, looking uncertain. Then he finally began to move toward the scattered seeds at the front of the room.

But Flo and Sam were already there. They paused for a moment, surveying the seeds, as if doing their best to memorize the individual types and determine how they were going to go about dividing their labor. This was one thing I didn't have as much control over as I would like—I could tell the pair I needed them to do something, but when it came who was actually going to do what, it was something they tended to manage on their own.

The two of them sat there for a moment, noses almost touching as they appeared to hash out their next step. As they were having their convo, Abigail's Chihuahua approached, ears flattened slightly, as if he was none too happy to see that the two tiny rodents had gotten there ahead of him. In fact, he bared his tiny teeth, and a low growl emerged from his throat.

I wanted to protest, to tell Professor Hendricks that Abigail needed to control her dog, but I remained silent. It was very, very rare for one familiar to attack another, and so I held back. If things got too tense, then I assumed the professor —or her robin—would step in.

Flo and Sam hurried away from the marauding Adolphus, taking up positions on the other side of the pile of seeds. From the opposite direction, Philippa's squirrel approached, tail still flicking away. The two gerbils sent one another a worried look, as though unsure whether they were about to get attacked from yet another quarter.

The squirrel came closer…and closer…and then settled down on his haunches, picked up a sunflower seed, and began munching on it.

A chuckle swept around the classroom.

"No, Mr. Butters!" Philippa moaned. "You're not supposed to *eat* them!"

Mona shot her teammate a glance of pure fury. "I knew I should have had Silas do this trial!"

"He wouldn't have done any better than Mr. Butters!" Philippa retorted.

"Girls," Professor Hendricks said in quelling tones. "Control yourselves."

The pair scowled at one another and then settled back in their seats, clearly seething. I wouldn't allow myself to smile, but I couldn't help being relieved that apparently Mr. Butters wouldn't be any kind of a threat in this particular competition.

That left Adolphus. The tiny dog and my two gerbils appeared to have reached some sort of *détente,* because he was busy trying to scoop up a sunflower seed with his little pink tongue while Flo and Sam used their tiny, clever hands to snatch up as many seeds as they could.

"One minute left," Professor Hendricks said.

The sour sensation returned to my stomach. I couldn't do anything except sit there, however, since any direct intervention on my part would lead to immediate disqualification. It looked as though the gerbils were doing well enough, but would they get back to my desk before the trial ended?

Meanwhile, Adolphus had apparently decided the only way he would get all the seeds back to his mistress in the time allowed was to scoop them up from the floor so he could carry them in his mouth. He nosed around on the floor, gathering seeds, and then, apparently satisfied, began to trot back toward his mistress.

At the same time, Flo and Sam turned away from the seed pile and hurried over to my desk.

They leapt up and caught the hem of my skirt with their teeth, and then scrambled onto the desktop.

"Ten seconds," said the professor.

Adolphus was also at his mistress's desk. She let him jump into her lap, and from there onto her desk. Once he was back on *terra firma*—relatively speaking, anyway—he opened his mouth and dropped a nasty-looking heap of saliva-covered grains and seeds on the scratched surface.

"Ew," Juno muttered under her breath.

I was inclined to agree. My gerbils' method was much neater.

They let go of the grains they were clutching and let them fall on my desk. Just a second later, Professor Hendricks intoned as her robin flew over to land on her shoulder,

"Time."

Abigail and I both sat with our hands folded in our laps, making sure there would be absolutely no question about any possible interference. The professor approached Abigail's desk first, and peered down at the soggy grains displayed there.

"Sunflower…yes…flax…wheat…rice…." She stopped there, the line between her brows deepening as she studied the collection Adolphus had retrieved. "There are two millet seeds here. Minus ten points."

This pronouncement made Abigail press her

lips together, but she didn't bother to protest, only sat there quietly. After all, the proof of her familiar's error was there for all to see—well, if they had very good eyesight. Those millet seeds were tiny.

Professor Hendricks straightened and came over to my desk. "Let us see how your familiars did."

Flo and Sam had remained sitting there while the professor performed her assessment of Abigail's familiar's work, but as soon as the professor approached, they fled for the safety of my cardigan pockets. No doubt they didn't much like being loomed over like that.

Once again, Professor Hendricks bent to study the collection of seeds, and once again she enumerated them slowly as she inspected my familiars' handiwork. Her expression didn't shift, but I thought I caught a glimpse of startled approval in her cool gray eyes.

"One of each seed—nothing missing, nothing beyond what was asked for," she said. "Very good. One hundred points for you and your team."

Juno opened her mouth as though she was about to let out a whoop of triumph...before realizing this probably wasn't the sort of place for that kind of display. Instead, she flashed me a quick grin, while Celeste and Helen exchanged looks of pure relief.

"The purpose of this exercise," Professor

Hendricks pronounced without missing a beat, "was to see how well your familiars can perform complicated tasks and follow orders. I know that you've been working closely with Professor Hamilton to make sure these are skills you all can master. While all the trials are being conducted in my classroom, I want to let you know that the professor will be informed as to how you performed in this task, just so she will know what to focus on for the remainder of the school year. Any questions?"

We all glanced at one another, but no one spoke. I got the feeling that the revelation about Professor Hamilton being told how our familiars had done wasn't precisely popular. Well, I could see why my fellow students might not be happy about that, but at the same time, I also understood why our Working With Familiars instructor would need to know how everyone had done so she could tailor her instruction to make it more effective.

"That is all for today," Professor Hendricks told us. "You may go."

Because that was one good thing about the days when we had these trials—once they were completed, we got to leave early. It might have been better if Beginning Spells had been the last class of the day, because then we would have been at liberty to do what we liked for the rest of the afternoon, rather than loiter around until it was time to go to Working With Familiars.

As it was, we all headed outside to get some fresh air, our familiars coming along as well, since they would be needed in our next class. Helen and Juno and Celeste and I went to our favorite spot, the little copse where we'd shared a picnic lunch with the boys from Master Marco's not so long ago. This was also a sunny, bright day, although, since it was barely ten o'clock in the morning, the air remained cool, with the full warmth of the day not due for several more hours.

"That was amazing!" Juno exclaimed. "See, I told you that you had nothing to worry about."

I shrugged, and reached inside my pockets so I could give the gerbils a little thank-you pat on the head. Once they were back in their cage, I'd give them a special treat as a further way of saying thanks.

"Yes, they did very well," Celeste agreed. "And those extra hundred points will definitely help."

"That's for sure," Helen said. "Especially after that last History of Magic test. I barely squeaked by with a C-minus."

The test had been a tough one, with a long essay requiring us to explain all the various ins and outs of how the Department of Magical Exile had come to be, but I'd acquitted myself well, and received an A-minus. Then again, history had always been one of my better subjects at secondary school. Memorizing facts was easy enough. Making magic actually work was an entirely different matter.

"Did you see Mona's face?" Juno asked next, brown eyes dancing with laughter. "I seriously thought her head was going to pop off her neck, she was so angry."

I reflected privately that our lives would all be much easier if Mona had managed to literally explode with rage, but I rather doubted that was going to happen any time soon. And honestly, I felt a bit bad about the way she had browbeaten her teammate. There was no love lost between Philippa Carmody and me, but no one deserved to be treated like that.

"Mona's the type who wants to be in control of everything," I said. "It was probably driving her mad to see Philippa's familiar fail so badly and not be able to do a single thing about it."

"Serves her right," Helen replied. "Maybe if she were a bit nicer, we wouldn't all be here crowing about how she lost."

This observation was nothing more than the truth, so I couldn't do much beyond nod in agreement. And I had to admit that it felt very good to finally have beaten Mona McGee at something.

If only I could be confident about our chances of repeating that particular feat.

CHAPTER 11
MIDSUMMER MUSINGS

As I'd guessed, our victory was short-lived. Of course, no one could take away the points we'd earned at the April trial—and I'd be the first to admit that they would help us enormously when it came time to calculate our end-of-year tally—but still, irritation flared at the end of May when, once again, Mona and her team managed to be victorious in that month's challenge. The task had been to levitate a stack of books off Professor Hendricks' desk, and this time it was Noreen Gillespie who'd competed, rather than Mona. However, unlike poor Philippa, Noreen had sailed through with flying colors—no doubt the reason why Mona had once again stepped aside to allow someone else to compete in her place.

Still, I couldn't be too glum, not when the

Midsummer ball was set to take place in less than three weeks. Lochlan and I had been writing the entire time, but naturally, being able to see each other in person was much better than exchanging dry words. We'd both agreed to keep the contents of our letters such that we wouldn't be embarrassed to have them read by a third party, since we didn't know for sure whether anyone from either school was looking at them before they were passed on to us.

His classes seemed to be going well enough, or at least, if Lochlan had his own failures at Master Marco's, he'd apparently decided to keep those failures to himself. Instead, he told me mainly about the pranks he and his classmates played on one another, and who had come out on top in that week's football match, and discussed with me what we wanted to do during those two glorious weeks in August when we wouldn't have any classes.

Apparently, Miss Primm and Master Marco had come to some sort of agreement about that particular situation, because it appeared they were going to allow the students from both schools to come and go freely during the fortnight between terms. Simply dreaming of so much freedom was enough to get my insides tingling with anticipation...assuming, of course, that I would pass with enough points to go on to my second year.

But I tried my best to put those niggling doubts aside and apply myself to my schoolwork. True, I turned Professor Hendricks' desk into a fairy ring of mushrooms when I was attempting to conjure a gold ring on my finger, and daisies had fallen from the ceiling in the middle of a spell to invoke a rainstorm, but still, things could have been much worse. I'd even managed to make a book disappear from my desk and appear in the library down the hall from our classroom, which meant my magic was there, even if it still was an unruly thing with no wish to be harnessed.

The solstice came, on a warm and lovely day that made me gladder than ever that Miss Primm had determined the dance would be held outside, under the stars. The same pavilion that had been used for our spring picnic was pressed into service again, only this time, magical fairy lights danced from the roof and all the sides were left open to the night air.

My green velvet gown wasn't a very good option for such a mild summer night, but Juno had come to my rescue there. She'd known that I wouldn't write home and ask my mother to send me something suitable for the occasion—not because we couldn't afford it, but because I knew my mother would view such a request as highly frivolous—and so my roommate had taken it upon herself to ask her own mother if she could send a few more dresses over.

"Just consider it a very late birthday present," Juno said breezily as I tried to tell her she shouldn't have gone to all that trouble. "Besides, I didn't want to think of you sweating in that green velvet gown all night. It's beautiful, but way too hot for this weather."

Since she was right, I held back my protests and thanked her for the gift. And the dress she'd gotten for me was beautiful—a dreamy color somewhere between soft blue and pale violet, with a cross-over bodice and a floaty skirt made of multiple layers of chiffon. I felt like a fairy princess in it, especially since Juno had also ordered a pair of silvery sandals to go along with the gown...sandals with minimal heels, as she knew all too well that if she tried to make me wear the sort of spikes she favored for special occasions, I'd fall flat on my face.

Wearing our finery, we all went out to the pavilion to meet our dates. A round yellow moon was rising behind the forest to the east, and enchanted lanterns hung in the air, marking our way.

"Do you ever think we'll be able to perform magic like that?" Helen asked wistfully as she glanced up at the lanterns.

"I'll settle for graduating," Juno said. "I don't

need to do anything fancy—I just want to make sure I get to stay here in this world instead of being shipped off to work in an office building or something."

"We have office buildings here, too," Celeste pointed out, and Juno quirked an eyebrow.

"Not the same thing."

Maybe it wasn't. My father went to work at DOME every day, and I knew his office was in a tall building of some sort, but no one could claim that his job was at all mundane.

Celeste's thoughts must have run along those same lines, because she didn't argue, only gave a shrug. When she spoke, her tone was thoughtful. "I suppose it is fun to daydream about controlling magic the way the professors here do, or even how others in our family can, but Juno is right—the most important thing is to do well enough that there is no question about us staying here in our world."

Helen nodded, although she looked a bit crestfallen. It was hard to put dreams aside, even when we all knew deep down that we'd never be accomplished magical practitioners.

It was hard to admit that one's greatest aspiration was to be merely adequate.

Subdued, we traversed the last few yards to the pavilion. Once we reached the huge tent, however, we were immediately cheered up, because Billy and Dev and Isaac and Lochlan were there, a bit more casual than at the Midwinter dance, since they'd left aside their dress coats and only wore vests and ties and crisp shirts with their dark slacks.

A few moments were spent in getting caught up, and then we paired off to either fetch some refreshments, as Billy and Helen did, or to move onto the dance floor, like Celeste and Isaac and Juno and Dev. Lochlan, on the other hand, only paused to fetch us a couple of cups of punch before leading me out of the pavilion and into the warm summer night.

"I didn't want to stay inside there with such a moon overhead," he told me, and I had to agree. Why trap yourself in a stuffy pavilion when there was a full midsummer moon to be seen?

"Yes, this is much better," I said.

Hand in hand, we walked across the lawn to the edge of the forest. We found a fallen log, and Lochlan carefully dusted it off with his hand as best he could before he allowed me to sit down.

"I didn't want to mess up that dress of yours," he said as I seated myself. "It's really pretty."

"Thanks," I said. "Juno got it for me. I wasn't going to bother my parents about getting me a new party dress, but she told me that friends don't let friends wear velvet in June."

Lochlan scrunched up his nose as he considered my statement. "Is that a fashion rule or something?"

"According to Juno, it is." I lifted my cup of punch and took a sip. It was lighter in color than the punch we'd had at midwinter, fizzy and tasting of citrus.

He chuckled and drank as well, but then paused to gaze down at me, as if trying to decipher my expression. "How are you holding up?"

"Just fine," I replied, and sent a quizzical glance back at him. "Haven't you been getting my letters?"

"I have," he said, "but we both know we're not telling the entire truth in those letters."

I let out a breath. "Well, I suppose things could be going better, but they could also be worse. Barring any huge catastrophes, we should be able to make it to our second year without too much trouble."

My comment made him grin, teeth flashing white in the moonlight. "That's the trick, isn't it? Especially when none of us can know for sure when our magic isn't going to go careening out of control like a car whose steering enchantments have worn off."

That was definitely one way to describe the sensation of watching a spell you'd thought would work go completely awry. About all I could do was smile in return. "And then there are two more years after this one, each progressively harder. Or at least, I assume they must be more difficult. We're not allowed to ask the second- and third-years about their coursework, so I don't know for sure." I sipped some more punch, then tilted my head up at Lochlan. "I don't suppose you have any insights."

"Unfortunately, no." He sat down next to me; the fallen log shifted slightly, but not enough that I needed to worry about getting dislodged. "Same rules at Master Marco's."

"I'm sort of surprised no one has said anything about Celeste seeing Isaac," I remarked next. "He's a year ahead of her, isn't he?"

"Yes, but maybe it's different because they're from two different schools." Lochlan's expression grew sly, and he added, "Or maybe it's because there are enchantments in place to silence people if they start talking out of turn."

I stared at him. "You really think that's true?"

"I don't know," he replied. "We have all kinds of spells and enchantments for so many other things. Why not that? It isn't even the sort of thing you'd realize existed until you tried to break the rules."

The more I thought about it, the more his theory made sense. Yes, the school was set up to keep the three years of students as physically sepa-rated as possible, but we still passed one another in the halls or in the stairwells, not to mention the way we were all seated together in the dining hall. Plenty of opportunities existed for people to be telling tales out of school…so to speak.

But if there existed spells to ensure that third-year students didn't tell second-year students what was coming, and so on down the line, then each new generation of students would have to learn the ropes for themselves.

"What kind of spell would it be, do you think?" I asked. "Something that would simply stop a person from saying anything at all, or one that would let Miss Primm or one of the professors know that a certain student wasn't following the rules?"

Lochlan considered my question for a moment before saying, "It's probably the former. Otherwise, don't you think they'd use that as a strike against you when it came to deciding whether you stayed or went?"

I hadn't even thought of that. A chill went over me, despite the warm summer night. It was really rather horrible to consider all the ways a student might be prevented from finishing their coursework at our schools, when you got right down to it.

Of course, the situation wasn't really quite so dire. It seemed clear enough to me the professors really were doing their best to make sure we gained the skills necessary to graduate and go on to normal, magical lives. Otherwise, it would have been far too easy for them to call us out for every single magical transgression and see that we were shipped off to Mundania immediately.

"But this is gloomy talk for a midsummer's night," Lochlan said. He set down his cup of punch and got to his feet, then extended a hand to me.

I took it, even as I said, "It seems silly to call this midsummer when it's really only the solstice. We have months and months of summer ahead of us still."

"And good thing, because I was certainly tired of winter. But what I'm most looking forward to is August." His eyes met mine, eager. "What do you want to do with all our free time?"

"Everything," I said simply, and he laughed.

"Could you narrow that down a bit?"

I sent him an impish look. "Well, then—picnics, and boating on the pond. And horseback riding. We have stables here, but I haven't had a chance to go riding yet. It's part of Physical Activities for the second- and third-year students, and only a special treat for us first-years."

"Do you ride?" Lochlan asked.

"Not at all," I confessed with a grin. "But I've always wanted to learn."

"Then you shall," he said. "We can learn

together, because I've never been on a horse before. I'll just have to hope the one I choose doesn't decide to throw me."

"I'm sure the horses at Miss Primm's are very well-behaved," I responded.

"Well, we'll find out." His fingers tightened on mine, and he pulled me closer. "I suppose we should go back soon so they don't send out search parties."

"I suppose," I echoed.

"I said 'soon,' not right away."

His eyes glinted in the moonlight, and he bent and kissed me, mouth sweet and tangy with punch. Was there anything better than moonlit midsummer kisses from Lochlan Abernathy?

I somehow doubted it.

But, true to his word, he led me back to the pavilion after that. All that walking and talking and kissing had definitely whetted my appetite, and I was happy to make a good dent in the refreshments that had been set out for us. We danced as well, and this time I could see Master Marco and Miss Primm clearly in the crowd. They stood off to one side, away from the refreshment table, and appeared to be holding some sort of intense conversation, since his head was bent down toward hers, and they spoke quickly, gazes moving constantly as though to make sure no one else was close enough to hear what they were saying.

Were they planning yet another gala? I hadn't heard that there were to be any more joint parties like this one, that July and the beginning of August were to be set aside for everyone to study and knuckle down as they prepared for their final exams. Once we were past those, of course, we'd have two glorious weeks of freedom, but even then, I got the impression that we students would be allowed to do as we wished, and that nothing terribly structured was planned.

I almost said something to Lochlan, but once the dance was over, we were met by our friends, and we all went to load up our plates with more treats from the refreshment tables, then headed off to one of the tables set outside so we could enjoy the moonlight and the cool nighttime breeze. It was good to see that everyone seemed to be getting along so well, and I wondered if our little octet would remain intact through the summer and on into the next two years of school.

"Master Marco and Miss Primm seem awfully chummy," Helen remarked as she reached for a petit four.

We all made noises of assent—even the boys, who generally weren't quite as perceptive about such things.

"Definitely looks like they're plotting something," Juno said. She'd just finished eating a sausage roll, and paused to wipe her fingers on the napkin she'd placed in her lap.

"Perhaps they're only planning for their time off this summer," I replied, thinking of how Lochlan and I had recently done that very same thing. "I'm sure they're looking forward to the break, just like the rest of us."

Dev ruffled a hand through his thick dark hair. "Do you think they even get one? I mean, they're still in charge, even if the rest of us get to lollygag for a couple of weeks."

"I think so," Celeste told him. "It sounds as though the professors take turns being in charge while the headmistress goes on holiday."

Which seemed like a reasonable arrangement to me, especially since, even though we were students here, we were also all adults, and therefore not quite the same responsibility as children under the age of eighteen. And after spending months forcing our unruly magic to behave itself even the littlest bit, I had a feeling that the students at the academy weren't going to be terribly inclined to experiment and get themselves in trouble.

Famous last words, but hope sprang eternal, I supposed.

"They do the same thing at our school," Lochlan said. "Maybe it's a little rough that the headmaster and all the students get two weeks off while the professors only get one, but I figure they must do something to compensate them for the time."

I hadn't really thought about that. Tuition at the two schools was free, because it had been determined when they were first established centuries earlier that no one should be barred from admittance simply because of an inability to pay. Unlike in Mundania, true poverty couldn't exist in a world where magic made everything so much easier, and yet our society still had its strata, those who lived in abundance while others eked out a much more modest existence.

"I'm sure Miss Primm is very happy that she and Master Marco will have the same two weeks off," Juno put in slyly, and everyone chuckled. While there definitely wasn't anything about their public behavior that appeared at all scandalous, it was still fairly easy to tell they shared some kind of attraction, even if they were doing their best to act circumspect.

What would come of it, I couldn't begin to guess.

After we were done with our snacks, Juno and Dev and Celeste and Isaac headed back to the dance floor, while Helen and Billy wandered off toward the school, where the full moon cast a welcoming light on the large terrace located at the back of the building. Lochlan and I lingered at the table for a moment, as if we'd both agreed that we wanted this time alone together.

"Two more months," he said, and a little thrill of uneasiness went over me. It was one thing to say I was doing well enough, that I really didn't have any reason to worry, but I didn't know for sure. Celeste and Helen had devised a complicated way of tracking all our tests and practicums, and so they predicted we should all be able to at least slide through at the end of the term.

But predictions were known to fail, and so much rested on my final exam in Beginning Spells. I wasn't worried about Physical Activity, because it was scored purely on a pass/fail basis, and even someone as clumsy as I could squeak by with a pass. The only way to really fail was to sit out the class entirely; I had a feeling the course had been included in the curriculum as a way to ensure easy points for even the most hapless students. Likewise, I was doing well in History of Magic, and although my attention wobbled a bit, I was also earning well above a passing grade in Focus and Concentration. Thanks to my bond with Flo and Sam, Working With Familiars wasn't any real concern, either.

Beginning Spells could be brutal, though. I could never tell from day to day whether a particular spell or exercise would succeed or would go

careening completely out of control, as Lochlan
had phrased it just an hour or so earlier. If I failed
spectacularly enough, even those extra points I'd
earned in the trial involving my familiars wouldn't
be enough to save me.

"Yes," I said in response to Lochlan's
comment, hoping I sounded sunny and not at all
worried about what would happen during those
two months. "It's hard to believe the term has
flown by so quickly."

He didn't say anything for a moment, as he
was busy studying my expression. "It's really going
to be all right, you know."

"I keep telling myself that, but...."

I didn't say anything else; there didn't seem to
be much reason to. In silence, Lochlan reached
out and took my hand, and I squeezed his fingers,
gladder than I could say about having him there
with me...about meeting him in the first place.
Yes, I could have gotten through all of this with
only my friends as moral support, and yet it still
felt even better to know Lochlan believed in me
and thought I would do just fine.

I would hate to disappoint him.

"I find it's always when you near the end that
it gets worse," he said quietly. "Up until that
point, I suppose you can keep telling yourself that
it's far off in the future and there's plenty of time
to get ready. But now we're at the point where it

feels as though it's all rushing toward us like a speeding train."

Yes, that was exactly how I felt. I knew there were still two months to go, but the last few weeks would be spent in review and study, not on learning anything new.

But in the meantime….

Still holding Lochlan's hand, I stood. "Let's go dance," I said.

Nothing more than that, but I had the idea he understood. I wanted to get moving and try to forget about the future for a bit.

"Absolutely," he replied.

Hand in hand, we walked back to the pavilion. Our friends greeted us, and soon enough, we lost ourselves in the music.

It was exactly what I needed.

CHAPTER 12

CANDLE TRICKS

The "speeding train" definitely increased its pace after that. I found it hard to concentrate when such wonderful warm summer days beckoned outside the windows of Miss Primm's academy, but at least the light lingered long enough that we still had time to wander the grounds and get some fresh air after classes were done for the day. Several times, our little group noticed a big black car leaving the academy's grounds and heading off in the direction of Master Marco's school, but—as Celeste pointed out—the other school was certainly not the only point of attraction which lay in that direction, and so it was a little silly to assume that Master Marco's had been the headmistress's destination on all of those occasions.

At least the trial at the end of June was our

final one for that first year; Professor Hendricks announced she would not hold one on July thirty-first, as we would be busy prepping for our exams, which would be held the week of August sixteenth. That was fine by me, since I didn't hold any great hope that my team would be able to prevail in whatever task she might devise to torture us.

Sure enough, when we filed into the classroom that last day of June, I saw a large collection of white pillar candles sitting on a table placed off to one side of Professor Hendricks' desk, and my heart sank. Throughout the year, we'd been working on summoning flame to light candles and set logs in a hearth ablaze, with varying success. Once, I'd actually managed to make a candle light simply by touching my finger to the wick...but only two weeks later when I'd attempted the same feat, the entire candle had melted into a puddle of wax at my touch.

Juno and Celeste had been successful in their attempts to light candles, while Helen had only summoned a faint smell of burning wax and nothing else. Clearly, either Celeste or Juno would need to represent our team on this one.

"Celeste had better do it," Juno said as we huddled together to plot strategy. "Yes, I've called the fire a couple of times, but there was that one time where the flame floated around in the air a while before it finally touched the wick, and I can just see me dropping it into the trash can or on the bookshelf or something else combustible. Celeste has more control."

We all looked at her, and she gave a resigned nod. "I suppose that makes sense," she said. "Even though I am not as sure of myself as you seem to think I am. But I will do my best."

"That's all we can ask," I told her.

"I'd say it is no problem, but I am not so sure of that." However, her chin was lifted, and she looked ready to do battle despite her reservations.

With that matter settled, we waited until Professor Hendricks called the team representatives up to her desk. To no one's surprise, Mona McGee was representing her team once again. Abigail Andrews had taken the lead for her team on this particular task, and Celeste went to stand near her.

"This challenge is simple enough," the professor said. "All you need to do is select a candle from the ones waiting on the table over there, set it on my desk, and call a flame to the wick. Once it's burned for thirty seconds, blow it out and put it back with the others."

"That's trust," Juno murmured in my ear. "I'm not sure I'd want students messing with fire anywhere near my desk."

Although I was inclined to agree, I only lifted

my shoulders. "It also raises the stakes," I replied in an undertone. "You know how she's told us over and over that we need to be able to stay cool in a crisis and not let what's going on around us get in the way of working our magic. She may very well want to see how our team leaders react if something goes wrong."

Professor Hendricks paused and sent a piercing stare in Juno's and my direction. "Is there something you girls would like to share with the rest of the class?"

"Um, no," I said hastily.

Was that a sniff I heard? Eyes narrowed, the professor replied, "Then please do us the courtesy of remaining silent while these students perform the task assigned them."

I pressed my lips together and shifted in my seat so I wasn't sitting right on the edge, then folded my hands demurely in my lap. Juno did much the same. Whether or not the professor was mollified by our show of cooperation, I couldn't tell for sure…but she did transfer her attention to the three girls standing up at the front of the classroom.

"Well, then," she said in a slightly louder voice. "Miss Saint-Michel, please fetch your candle and set it on the desk."

With a nod, Celeste did as requested, then went ahead and put the white pillar candle down on Professor Hendricks' desk in an open spot near the front.

"Now, light it."

Celeste had never been the type to show much anxiety in a given situation, and clearly, she didn't intend to start now. Coolly, she stood there for a moment, gazing at the candle, most likely rehearsing the spells we'd used to summon fire. Once such a spell was written in one's mind, it wasn't necessary to recite it aloud, but only to go through the syllables in one's head. However, the professor had assured us it was also acceptable to say the words out loud until we were comfortable with mental spells.

It seemed Celeste had decided to go the safer route, because she pulled in a little breath, then said,

"Banish dark
Light again
Candle bright
Bring your flame!"

The wick on her candle began to smolder. Juno and Helen and I watched it, breathless, all of us repeating whatever prayers we knew under our breath so the wick would truly catch and display the kind of flame the professor was asking for.

But then the tiny red glow vanished, and a trail of thin smoke began to rise from the candle.

Juno muttered something under her breath, even as my heart sank.

So close…but not good enough.

"Thank you, Miss Saint-Michel," said Professor Hendricks coolly. "You may take your seat now."

Celeste's only answer was a nod. She came down the aisle to seat herself at the desk behind mine, chin held high, expression steady. I knew she must have been disappointed, but one certainly couldn't tell by looking at her.

"Miss Andrews?" the professor said next.

Abigail stepped forward, selected her own candle, and put it on the desk. Apparently deciding that it wasn't a good idea to mirror what Celeste had done, she instead performed the spell silently, although her lips moved enough for everyone to tell what she was doing.

And nothing happened, not even the tiny spark that had begun to smolder in the wick of Celeste's candle before it put itself out.

For a long moment, Abigail remained where she was, fingers knotted in the wool of her plaid skirt. Her lips moved again, and I guessed she was trying desperately to get the thing to light. Unfortunately, it remained stubbornly dark, and at length, Professor Hendricks spoke.

"You may sit down, Abigail."

That was all she said, but it was enough.

Clearly, she wasn't about to allow a single student to stand there and waste time by making the same futile attempt over and over.

Face white, Abigail headed back to her seat. Her teammates uttered quiet words of sympathy, but I got the impression that they were just as frustrated as the rest of us.

However, all was not lost. Professor Hendricks had told us at the start that if none of the three teams were able to successfully complete a task, then its points would be rewarded equally to everyone. If Mona failed—and I hadn't once seen her able to successfully summon fire—then at least we'd get some points, if not anything even close enough to catch up to her team.

She seemed confident enough as she walked over to the table and made rather a show of selecting a candle. It appeared to be one that had been used in other exercises such as this, since the wick was buried deeply within the wax, seeming to indicate it had endured a good many hours of burn time already.

After she set it down on the professor's desk, Mona took a step back and stared at the candle for a moment, her hands buried in the pockets of her cardigan, as though contemplating the task ahead of her. A little smile played on her thin lips. Was she anticipating yet another win, or was she merely toying with us, trying to make us think she could manage this feat easily even though we all knew she was terrible at summoning fire?

And then the candle began to glow, flickering slightly as the buried wick came to life.

Darn it.

"Very good, Miss McGee," Professor Hendricks said. "Now, extinguish the flame."

Almost at once, the candle went dark. Mona picked it up and returned it to the table with the rest of its companions, then went back to her seat.

"And that is the conclusion of this year's trials," the professor informed us…as if we didn't already know. "Mona McGee's team finishes with five hundred points, and Celeste Saint-Michel's with one hundred points. These points will be added to your term-end totals, and will be used to calculate your final examination scores. Thank you for your hard work, everyone."

With that, she dismissed us, and we all gratefully escaped the classroom so we could soak up some welcome July sun before heading off to our Working With Familiars class. As we went, however, I noticed Mona fingering an odd rectangular object in her pocket, something that disappeared in a glint of silver even as I stared at her.

What in the world was that thing? It didn't even look truly metallic, but more as though its silvery color was something that had been painted on. Not a piece of jewelry, then. Some kind of odd good-luck charm?

That might explain her winning streak. As Celeste and Helen and Juno and I gathered outside to wait for our next class, I mentioned the strange object I'd seen, and also my speculation that it might be a good-luck charm.

"Those aren't allowed," Helen said, her tone flat. "That's why we can't bring anything except clothes with us, not even jewelry. I heard that back in the day, people were smuggling in all sorts of charms to give them an edge and help them earn enough points to move on to the next year of school."

"It would make sense," Juno said. Her dark eyes looked flinty, and I could tell she was less than pleased by the possibility that Mona McGee had been gaming the system by using some kind of illicit good-luck charm. "I mean, the girl is hopeless, so how is it possible that she could have won so many of the trials this year?"

Celeste frowned slightly. "We would need to have much more evidence than this in order to say anything to Professor Hendricks...or to Miss Primm."

"I know what I saw," I said, although possibly those words were a bit disingenuous. Honestly, I didn't know *exactly* what I'd seen, only that it had been...something.

Judging by Celeste's dubious expression, she thought my evidence was flimsy at best. "Enough that you're willing to go to the professor about it?"

"Probably not," I admitted, and Juno let out an annoyed hiss of a breath. "Still," I went on before she could say anything else, "I'm going to be keeping an extra-close eye on Mona from now on."

"What good is *that* going to do?" Helen asked plaintively. "The competitions are over. Even if she was cheating somehow, there's no reason for her to keep on cheating, not now. She has enough points from the tasks that even if she barely passes the exams, she's going on to next year."

I had to admit that was true. And honestly, even though Mona McGee was definitely not on my list of favorite people, I hadn't seen any real evidence of her cheating on any of our monthly or midterm tests. Like me, she seemed to be clever enough when it came to essays and multiple choice exams...more's the pity, because that would have made it more difficult for her to cheat her way into a second year at the academy.

"It never hurts to keep an eye on people you don't trust," Juno said. "Even if you don't have anything you can specifically pin on them at the moment."

Helen bit her lip, and Celeste continued to regard me with a slightly raised eyebrow, indicating that she thought I was making mountains out of molehills.

And maybe I was. I couldn't even say for sure why one small glimpse of an object I couldn't completely identify had raised my hackles so much, but I thought I'd go ahead and listen to my instincts, even if some of my friends weren't yet on board with my suspicions.

We had to head off to Working With Familiars after that, and so the topic was tabled for the time being. However, when we got to class, I noticed right away how Mona wore a smirk that seemed to indicate she thought she'd gotten away with something.

Then again, it could have been merely my imagination, and the only reason she was looking pleased with herself was that she'd managed to win the final trial for her team, and now had very little to worry about when final exams rolled around. I had to admit there was a distinct possibility I might have worn a similar expression if I'd been in her position.

But still…it bothered me.

J uly was a blur of studying and doing our
best to practice the bits and pieces where
we thought we'd be most challenged by our
final exams—me with my spellwork, Juno
and Celeste in History of Magic, Helen in
working with the little banty rooster who was her
familiar. I thought it actually did help somewhat
to be so focused and not get distracted by
Professor Hendricks' monthly trials, and so I was
glad I didn't have to worry about one coming up
at the end of the month.

And—although I didn't like to admit such a
thing to myself—it was also something of a relief
to know I wouldn't get to see Lochlan until mid-
August. When we had special occasions like
Midsummer balls and springtime picnics popping
up in the schedule, I tended to pay far more atten-

tion to those standout events than to the real task at hand, which was making sure I had enough of a handle on my magic that I wouldn't be shuttled off to Mundania before I finished my entire three years at Miss Primm's.

Even so, as the fateful week of August sixteenth approached, I found myself wondering if all of it would be enough. By some miracle, I hadn't managed to blow anything up or turn my hair green or summon bands of marauding badgers to roam the halls of the academy, but just because I'd avoided such mishaps so far didn't mean they might not still be lurking in the future, just waiting to pounce while I was in the midst of my exams.

I'd also done my best to watch Mona and detect if she did anything suspicious, but so far, my surveillance had yielded very little. She still wore that secret little smirk from time to time, and yet I doubted any court of law would convict someone simply for wearing an unpleasant expression far too often. I certainly never caught another glimpse of the strange rectangular object she'd slipped into her pocket, or anything else I couldn't explain.

One day when we were all sitting in Celeste and Helen's room, doing our best to study despite the lure of the warm breeze and bright, sunny afternoon outside the windows, Helen closed her book with a sigh.

"I know I'll never be able to remember all this," she said. "It would be so much easier if our final exams were team efforts, just like the trials in Professor Hendricks' class."

I tilted my head at her. "I thought you said you were doing all right in History of Magic."

"I thought I was," she replied, and gave another dramatic sigh. "But reading through all of this instead of having it presented in shorter bits is making my head hurt. Right now, I can't keep Cletus the Elder and Cletus the Younger apart, and I certainly can't remember which spells they invented."

"Cletus the Elder created the light-casting spell," I said. "It was his son who invented permanence, so the spell would last exactly as long as the spell-caster wished."

"You see?" Helen required rhetorically of the universe. "I can't keep so many facts in my head at the same time. And really, what does knowing that do to help any of us with magic? It feels like useless information to me."

I was of the opinion that no information was useless, but I guessed that trying to argue with Helen in her current mental state probably wasn't the best idea. Instead, I closed my own book and said, "I think we should all go for a walk. It'll help to clear out some of the cobwebs."

All three of my friends looked measurably cheered up by that suggestion, and so we abandoned our texts and our spell scrolls—and even our familiars, since right then they felt like just another adjunct to the tests looming in less than a week.

"It really is brutal that they make us study like this in the middle of summer," Juno remarked as we left the cool, quiet halls of the academy's manor house behind and emerged into the bright sunshine of an August afternoon. The air was thick with the scent of warm grass, birds sang from the trees, and brightly colored butterflies fluttered near the rosebushes that bloomed in the gardens surrounding the building. We students were allowed to pick several roses a week to brighten our rooms, but the bushes were still thickly covered with flowers.

"I know," I said. "But I suppose they didn't want us to run riot for a full two months between terms, and it's not as though we'd be able to go home."

She frowned. "No, the Source forbid that we should be able to see our families, or go shopping or out to a restaurant or a club or—"

"Exactly," I cut in, interrupting what I could tell was going to be another of Juno's rants. Of all of us, she seemed to have the most difficulty following the academy's rules. That might have been because she was American, and therefore had been raised in a more permissive environment, or it could have been simply her free-spirited nature trying to assert itself. Either way, the farther we'd progressed into the summer months, the more she reminded me of a big cat trapped in a cage at the zoo, gorgeous and restless. "The rules are in place for a reason," I went on. "We need all our focus to be on what we're doing here, not going to parties or the cinema or whatever."

"Maybe," she grumbled, before adding, "although I think there are quite a few people who might say it's better to blow off some steam every once in a while. Otherwise, you can explode."

"There's no need to explode," Celeste said. "Not when our exams start next Monday. You only need to hold on for a few more days."

Juno settled into a grumpy silence after that, although she cheered up a bit when we all moved on to talking about our plans with the boys from Master Marco's school, and whether we should try horseback riding first or leave that as the big finish to our two weeks of utter hedonism.

"Better leave it for last," she said. "It would stink to get thrown from a horse our first day out and be laid up for the next two weeks."

That was something I hadn't really thought of.

True, the school could always call in someone who specialized in healing magic to take care of any injuries that might occur during the summer holidays, and yet I wondered if Miss Primm would go to those lengths if the mishap involved a simple broken leg or arm. She might consider it an object lesson in not taking too many unnecessary risks.

But no, such benign neglect didn't seem like something she would practice. I'd be the first to agree that the headmistress was not the sort to mingle much with her students, other than making announcements at mealtimes, and yet she'd always appeared friendly enough, offering a smile if she passed us by in the corridor, occasionally observing classes and making helpful suggestions. I doubted very much that she'd allow someone to sit in their room with a broken leg rather than being allowed to enjoy the few weeks of holiday we were given each year.

Still, it seemed my friends were in agreement with Juno, because both Celeste and Helen said waiting sounded like a good idea, and that it would probably be better to start out with picnics and gathering wildflowers—and perhaps a quiet row on the pond in one of the rowboats the school owned—and leave horseback riding for the grand finale, as it were.

With the matter settled—and with our spirits lighter after spending a good hour or so out of doors—we headed back to the school. The daylight would linger for quite some time, but dinner was always at six no matter what the time of year, and we didn't want to miss our evening meal. Studying—and roaming around outside—worked up a good appetite.

Four days to go.

OUR FINAL EXAMS WEREN'T HELD IN THE SAME order that classes had taken place during the year, mainly because the other two years had to take their finals in that same week, and so there was a bit of juggling to get everything to fit properly. That was why we all ended up out on the football field early on Monday morning, running through the exercises to prove that our time in Physical Activities had been of some benefit.

We played one round of football and then ran through a fairly tame obstacle course, with hoops to jump through and ropes to climb—not overly long ones, just enough to hoist ourselves over a low wall. And with those tasks managed, Professor Crenshaw gathered us together to inform us everyone in the class had passed.

This didn't come as much of a surprise to any of us, but it was still something of a relief to know those points would be added to our tallies, and that we could go on to our next final with a light heart.

Or somewhat light, at any rate, since the next exam was in History of Magic. I told myself I had nothing to worry about, but I could tell that Helen and Celeste and Juno were feeling otherwise.

"If it were simply regurgitating facts," Celeste said, "I would not be so anxious. But Professor Simms will grade us on our grammar as well, and that puts anyone who is not a native speaker of English at a disadvantage."

"You speak English perfectly," Juno pointed out, but Celeste only shook her head.

"Speaking and writing are not the same thing at all."

None of us could really argue with that statement, and so we settled for making reassuring noises, since there wasn't much else we could really do. I didn't know why the professors wouldn't make allowances for students who traveled to our school from other countries and who hadn't grown up speaking English. It didn't seem fair to me. But I suppose they'd decided that since they were the ones hosting the students, it was up to them to make the rules. At any rate, I knew Celeste was somewhat at a disadvantage, despite being very clever.

The test felt horribly long, with two hundred

multiple-choice questions and two essays of no shorter than a thousand words each. I sat at my desk in Professor Simms' classroom, magical quill pen that would never run out of ink scratching furiously away in the exam book I'd been given, and hoped I wasn't making some sort of horrible blunder. Was it really Josephine Picard who'd invented the magically powered furnace, or Jonas Picoult? And had the wizard wars between Luxembourg and Malta taken place in 1530, or 1630?

My brain felt as though it had been cudgeled one too many times to produce the correct answers, and it was with an odd mixture of weary relief and growing trepidation that I handed over my exam book to the professor when she came down the aisle to collect everyone's tests. I couldn't quite keep my stomach from clenching as I worried whether I'd gotten enough answers right to keep me in school, or whether I'd failed so miserably that they would toss me out before even giving me a chance to move on to my finals in Working With Familiars and Beginning Spells.

No, that wasn't right. I supposed it might have happened in the past, but I'd honestly never heard of a student being exiled to Mundania before they were even given a chance to finish all their final exams. That horrible day might still be coming, but at the very least, it wouldn't arrive until after I'd taken my Beginning Spells final.

Test days were half days, so once we were done with History of Magic, we all convened in the dining hall for lunch. As we sat down, Juno announced, "No talking about the test and comparing answers. If I screwed up horribly, then I don't want to know until I get my scores from Professor Simms. At least that way, I'll have a few days of blissful ignorance."

Since I'd been thinking almost the same thing, I nodded. "Good idea. Besides, there's no point in second-guessing ourselves. It's not as if we can go back and change what we wrote."

Helen took a large bite of her chicken salad sandwich, then washed it down with some lemonade. "I agree," she said. "I mean, if we had some way of turning back time and going back to fix our answers, that would be one thing. But that's one spell I definitely know better than to attempt."

As did the rest of us. Time magic was ridiculously complicated—and dangerous, because anyone who practiced it ran the risk of altering their own past and quite possibly erasing themselves from existence. In fact, some countries—England included—had banned it altogether, saying it allowed far too many opportunities for abuse and misuse. Anyone caught using it had their memory taken away and was immediately banished to Mundania, a punishment daunting enough that no one had been prosecuted for that particular crime in my entire lifetime.

We all made various noises of assent to Helen's remark and went back to eating our lunch. In the corner of my eye, I noticed Mona McGee laughing and chatting in an almost ostentatious fashion at a table a few feet away. Did she think she'd done especially well on the History of Magic exam, or did she simply want everyone to think that she had?

Either way, I wasn't going to allow myself to expend much emotional energy on her. With all her bonus points from the various trials her team had won, she knew she was in an enviable position, and only had to pass her other tests with the barest minimum to ensure she moved on to a second year.

Our tests the next day would be Focus and Meditation and Working With Familiars. I was glad they'd been scheduled in that order, because it meant I'd have a chance to get myself well and truly grounded before I was called on to demonstrate my ability in working with Flotsam and Jetsam.

As it turned out, the Focus final wasn't terribly difficult. Professor Chopra asked us all to sit on the floor in the lotus position and breathe deeply and evenly, and then work on consciously slowing our respiration and blood pressure. As we followed her instructions, she walked among us, hands slightly outstretched, as though she was using them to measure our breathing and heart rate. Actually, I had no doubt that was exactly what she was doing—it might have been a subtle form of magic, but no less valuable for that.

This went on for nearly an hour. By the end of that time, my legs felt as though they were going to remain locked in the lotus position permanently, but I hung on, doing my best to ignore the discomfort, and making sure my breathing stayed as even as possible.

Finally, though, Professor Chopra beamed at us and said, "Excellent, girls. There are a few of you who could use a little more work in this area —but I won't name names. You will know the results of this final when the end-of-term scores are tallied on Thursday."

I wished she had scrupled to name names. At least that way, I would've known how much harder I needed to try for my two remaining finals. True, that might not have been the best way to look at the situation, but I was already worried enough about the Beginning Spells examination. It would have helped to know whether everything was riding on it.

Since I wasn't to be allowed that glimpse of

my future, I had to be content with painfully unbending my legs and gratefully rising to my feet. Everyone seemed to be in a fairly good mood, which seemed to indicate we all thought we'd done well enough with the exercise that we weren't in danger of jeopardizing our end-of-term scores.

After a brief break so we could go back to our rooms and fetch our familiars, the girls in our class all trooped down to the conservatory where Professor Hamilton was waiting for us, her gorgeous wolf familiar lying in a couched position near her feet. She smiled at us, perhaps in an attempt to ease some of our worries about the upcoming examination.

"Good morning, everyone," she said. "I hope you are all rested and ready to go?"

I couldn't be sure about "rested"—my legs were still aching after sitting for more than an hour in a lotus position. Still, the Focus and Meditation exam hadn't been exactly what one could call mentally taxing, so I supposed I needed to hope for the best. At any rate, Flo and Sam were definitely in fine form for their final, considering they'd spent most of the morning sleeping while I was bending my legs into pretzel shapes.

Everyone murmured their assent, and the professor nodded. "Good. Your test today will be an extension of the exercises we've been working on all year. You will need to demonstrate your ability to communicate with your familiar, and to have your familiar carry out a series of simple tasks. Points will be deducted each time your familiar disobeys, or you don't successfully relay what he or she is seeing. Any questions?"

We all looked at one another, but even Juno seemed subdued. Rather than have her hand shooting up as was often the case during class, she stood quietly next to me, Fred perched on her shoulder, while she silently stared at Professor Hamilton. Judging by the expression on my friend's face, I got the feeling that she very much wished she was a mind reader so she could delve into the professor's thoughts and see what she had planned for us.

But while magic flourished in our world, there were very few people who could actually see another's thoughts or emotions, and definitely none of us magical misfits had that sort of rare skill. We would have to do this the hard way.

It seemed Professor Hamilton was going to run us through our paces in alphabetical order, because the first person she called was Abigail Andrews. She stepped forward, her little Chihuahua Adolphus trotting along beside her. His ears and tail were up, and it looked as though neither of them was too worried about the trial ahead.

"Abigail," Professor Hamilton said. "And Adolphus. Your test will be in two parts. Abigail, you need to have your familiar go into the conservatory and locate the miniature teacup I've left under the ficus lyrata plant. Have him bring it back to you. Once he's done that, have him tell you at least three types of flowers he saw on his way to and from the tree. Understand?"

Abigail nodded, but I saw the way she swallowed. Was it possible she wasn't quite as confident in her familiar's ability to complete the task as she wanted us to believe?

However, she didn't say anything, only picked up Adolphus and cuddled him for a moment before she set him back down on the ground and gave him a pat on the head. Soon after, he trotted off into the verdant depths of the conservatory, while we all stood there and waited.

And waited.

There weren't any clocks in the place, so I had no idea how much time passed. It felt excruciatingly long, though, and—judging by the way Abigail plucked nervously at the hem of her skirt as she stood there, watching for her little dog to return—it must have felt twice as bad to her.

At last, Professor Hamilton said, "I'm afraid your time is up. Perhaps you should go fetch your familiar."

"I hope he isn't hurt—" Abigail ventured, but the professor only shook her head.

"If he had injured himself somehow, he would have barked or made some sort of sound. I fear he is lost. Please go and find him."

The words were phrased as a request, but I could tell Professor Hamilton wasn't going to allow any protests. Abigail ducked her head and went off into the greenery, calling, "Adolphus! *Adolphus!*" as she went.

Next up was Lois Bradford, whose familiar was a large parrot who always tended to give Juno's Fred contemptuous glances, as if he thought any bird the size of a budgie was of no real use. Their task was to retrieve a ring that the professor had hidden at the top of one of the palm trees at the far edge of the conservatory, a task the large showy bird had no problem completing. Lois smiled faintly as she went to stand off to one side, the parrot sitting on her shoulder and looking smug.

Just as Lois and her bird were taking their place among the rest of us students, Abigail emerged from the greenery, Adolphus tucked under one arm. The dog was panting but looked otherwise unharmed.

"Everything all right?" Professor Hamilton inquired.

"I think so," Abigail replied, although her

voice quavered a bit. It had to have been quite a blow to have her familiar fail so spectacularly, especially when the two of them in general seemed to work well together.

"Very good," the professor said. Her gaze turned toward me. "Callie Dobkins."

My stomach plummeted to roughly the level of my shoes. With Flo and Sam riding on my shoulder—because it was too warm to wear a cardigan, and my skirt didn't have pockets—I stepped forward and did my best to look unconcerned. "Yes, Professor Hamilton?"

Her mouth lifted slightly. "Your task is similar, Callie. Have your familiars find where I've hidden a red ribbon tied to one of the pear trees. They will need to bring it back to you, and then let you know what they saw on their journey."

I nodded. On the surface, the task didn't seem too terribly difficult, but working with one's familiars wasn't always a cut-and-dried sort of situation. I knew they were trying to train us so such tasks would be as easy as breathing, but—as poor Abigail Andrews' experience had just shown—it wasn't quite that simple.

But I held Flo and Sam for a moment, and told them they needed to find the red ribbon Professor Hamilton had spoken of, and also that they had to bring it back to me. I wouldn't task them with telling me about the flowers they would see coming and going, because I knew that would only confuse them. It was better to wait until I could commune with them when they returned, and see what I could pick up from their minds.

As soon as they understood what was required of them, they scampered off into the greenery. I found I couldn't quite look at anyone as I waited for the gerbils to return; I didn't want to see the sneer on Mona's face, or the worry on Juno's…or the way Abigail appeared as though she was holding back tears while she clutched her little dog. All of that would only serve as a distraction.

The minutes felt as though they ticked by very slowly. My heartbeat sounded far too loud in my ears, even though I was standing there calmly and doing nothing to exert myself.

At last, though, Flo and Sam reappeared, hurrying toward me as they carried a bit of red ribbon in their teeth, stretched between them like the ribbon at a cutting ceremony. They dropped the ribbon at my feet and then jumped up to catch the hem of my skirt. From there, I gathered them both in my hands, holding them close and doing my best to see something of what they'd done.

Yes, that was the two of them scurrying along between the conservatory's various flowering plants, headed toward one of several pear trees growing in large tubs. Along the way, they passed azaleas and roses and lilies, as well as some cheerful pansies in pots.

I related all this to Professor Hamilton, who accepted the information with a smile and said, "Very good, Callie. You can go join the others who've completed their tasks."

About all I could do was nod, then go and stand next to Lois, whose parrot did not seem overly thrilled to have a couple of gerbils in such close proximity. To my relief, though, he didn't make any move toward them, but only remained on Lois's shoulder and occasionally preened his feathers with his sharp beak.

It felt strange to stand on the sidelines and watch everyone else be put through their paces. Juno and Fred did very well, and soon enough, she'd taken her place next to me, her entire stance one of utter relief. Helen's little banty rooster, Ajax, at first didn't seem to understand what was expected of him, but eventually he, too, acquitted himself by finding the little figurine of a chick that the professor had hidden in one of the large tubs of flowering plants.

Mona and her rat, on the other hand, were complete failures. Like Abigail's dog Adolphus, Silas the rat disappeared into the depths of the conservatory and had to be hunted down by his mistress, whose forbidding brows seemed to signal she was less than pleased with his performance.

But Celeste and her cat Mignon did well, and so did Mona's friend Philippa, whose squirrel Mr. Butters accomplished the task given them in what seemed like record time. If these had been team competitions, that might have been enough to put them over the edge. As it was, I had to wonder if all the other points Mona had racked up over the year would be enough to compensate for her utterly dismal performance with her familiar.

At the end, Professor Hamilton said, "Very good work, girls. I will tally your scores and send them on to Miss Primm, who will be doing the final collating. Overall results will be posted Thursday morning."

Nothing we didn't already know, but of course, no one would speak up to tell the professor such a thing. At the end, we all thanked her and filed out, and heaved a sigh of collective relief.

One more final to go…and it would be the worst one yet.

I didn't sleep well that night, which I suppose was understandable. Normally, the world went black almost as soon as my head hit the pillow, and I had no problem sleeping the allotted eight hours…and was happy with nine on the weekends. This time, though, I kept having nightmares of setting Professor Hendricks on fire or opening up horrible black voids that seemed determined to suck everything in their paths into their angry maws. Oh, and then there was the dream about turning Juno into a chicken. Why a chicken, I wasn't sure, although I supposed it probably had something to do with watching Helen put her rooster through its paces just that morning.

If the bleary eyes and yawns I saw around me at breakfast were any indication, I wasn't the only one who'd spent a difficult night. We weren't given coffee at the academy, only tea, a fact Juno decried for what felt like the hundredth time.

"And you call yourselves a civilized country," she grumbled as she dunked a tea ball in and out of her mug of hot water over and over again.

"We *are* civilized," I said mildly. It seemed obvious enough to me that Juno was determined to be in a bad mood, and so I didn't want to quarrel with her right before our exam. "And there is plenty of coffee to be had in England. I have absolutely no idea why Miss Primm doesn't have it here."

"It's probably just as well," Helen put in. "We don't want everyone completely crazy on caffeine, after all."

"Tea has caffeine," I pointed out.

"But not as much."

Since that was a simple truth, there didn't seem to be much value in arguing the topic further. I only nodded and drank some of my own tea, glad that my parents had never been much of ones for coffee, and so I'd never developed a taste for the stuff…and therefore couldn't really miss it.

We subsided into silence after that, each of us absorbed in eating our breakfast and, most likely, trying to see if we could possibly figure out what Professor Hendricks had planned for us that morning. She'd said very little about the final exam, other than telling us all she wouldn't test us on anything that hadn't already been covered in class, but since that particular class had been held for the greater part of ten months, it still left an enormous amount of material to cover.

Well, I'd already told myself—over and over again—that I could only do my best. If the universe intended other things for me—namely, a life in Mundania—then I supposed I would just have to make the best of it.

Of course, all that sounded very calm and mature...which was about the opposite of how I felt as I walked through the doors of Professor Hendricks' classroom that morning. Although we'd worked with our familiars in Beginning Spells previously, we had been told we were not to bring them to the final exam, since we'd already been tested on our ability to work with familiars in Professor Hamilton's class the day before.

I wished Professor Hendricks hadn't made that mandate. Even if I wasn't going to work directly with Flo and Sam, it still would have been a comfort for them to be with me. I would have even perspired while wearing my cardigan if it had meant I could have my two furry familiars nestling in its pockets.

But it was not to be. I sat down at my desk, and Juno and Helen and Celeste took their seats as well. All around us, our other classmates sat in their usual places. Everyone looked pale and strained, even those whose complexions shouldn't have allowed for such a thing. I had a feeling the same thought was rattling around in all our brains.

Who among those sitting here today might not be around after tomorrow?

Helen was biting her lip, as usual, and I had to force myself not to do the same thing. Throughout most of the year, I'd tried my hardest not to think too much about my family, since I'd known doing so would only make me homesick— and also ratchet up my anxiety, as letting my thoughts dwell on my mother and father and brother and sisters would only make me wonder how much of a disappointment I was to all of them.

Now, though…now it was harder than ever to prevent myself from brooding over what it must mean to them to have a daughter or sister at Miss Primm's, with the constant threat of banishment hanging over her head. I wondered if my father knew Mona McGee's father well, and whether the two men had made a pact to have the other man take on the unpleasant task of exiling his co-work-er's daughter to a world with no magic if she should fail.

My stomach roiled. Perhaps I shouldn't have had a third piece of bacon with breakfast. At the time, I'd thought that having some extra protein could only do me good while taking my final exam later that morning, but now I was beginning to believe it might have been better if I'd been abstemious and only had a fried egg and some fruit.

Well, it couldn't be helped now.

Professor Hendricks swept into the room. All right, perhaps she entered normally, but my mind had assigned so much importance to this day that it felt as if she'd swept in, her simple black wool skirt swishing as though it had been made of taffeta. I shifted in my seat, and many others must have as well, since a definite rustle went through the classroom as she took her place in front of her desk.

"Good morning, everyone," said the professor, as if this was just another ordinary day in Beginning Spells, rather than the one that might very well determine whether we'd be able to move on to our next year at Miss Primm's or be exiled forever. "I have decided that I will administer the practical exams in reverse alphabetical order. However, to begin, we will have a written test which will take approximately thirty minutes."

Another rustle moved through the class. We'd all known part of the test would be written, but those whose names fell toward the end of the alphabet were probably disheartened that they would have to step up first, rather than watch as the rest of us made our best attempts at practical magic.

Professor Hendricks extracted a stack of papers from a desk drawer and then proceeded to distribute them amongst us students. I took mine from her and told myself this was the easy part; memorizing spells and chants was simple enough for me. It was getting them to actually work in the real world that gave me so much trouble.

I took my pen and waited, knowing I couldn't start until the professor had given us the signal. Once all the tests had been handed out and she'd resumed her stance in front of her desk, she said, "You may begin."

Oddly, now that the moment was upon me, I felt almost calm. And, to be fair, the hardest part of this exam would be the practicum.

As Professor Hendricks had said, nothing was on the test that hadn't been covered in class. That was why I could write out the charm for be-spelling a broom for ordinary housework without any trouble, and then come up with two alternates for a spell to draw luck to the witch casting it. My pen scratched its way across the paper, and in fact, I finished all the questions several minutes before she spoke.

"The thirty minutes are up. Please put down your pens."

Everyone laid their pens down on their desk-tops and folded their hands while the professor walked amongst us, gathering our written tests. I risked a brief glance over at Juno, and she lifted her shoulders in a shrug. Presumably, that meant she thought she'd done all right but wasn't quite sure.

I nodded slightly, the only response I thought I could make without drawing down the profes-sor's ire. She went back to her desk, the stack of written exams in her hand, and placed them in the same drawer where she'd gotten them from originally. After that, she came back around to the front of her desk and sent us all an expectant look. "Very well, then," she said. "Time to move on to the practicum. Lydia Vronsky?"

Lydia was a pale, thin girl who looked perpet-ually startled. Even though Professor Hendricks had said she would be going through the practical tests in reverse alphabetical order, Lydia appeared even more shocked to be called on first. Her eyes widened, and she sat frozen in her seat for a moment, as though she hoped if she didn't respond right away, the professor might move on to someone else and forget she even existed.

Unfortunately, our Beginning Spells professor was not the sort of person to forget anything. She stood at the front of the class, hands planted on her black-clad hips, and continued to stare at poor

Lydia until the girl finally got out of her seat and made her way to stand next to Professor Hendricks' desk.

"Very good," the professor said. Possibly her mouth quirked just the slightest bit, but otherwise, she remained expressionless. "Your task, Miss Vronsky, is to turn the water in this vase blue."

From nowhere, Professor Hendricks' produced a large clear glass vase and set it down on her desk. Lydia gazed at it for a moment, eyes still wide.

"Any time now, Miss Vronsky."

Another long pause. Lydia stammered, "C-can I touch it?"

"Will that help?"

Lydia hesitated. "I-I'm not sure."

"Whatever you would like, Miss Vronsky."

My fellow classmate stepped up to the vase and laid both hands on it, cupping the curved surface. She took a deep breath and closed her eyes, and appeared to murmur something under her breath. Faint tendrils of soft turquoise began to swirl within the clear water, growing and widening until all the liquid inside the vase had turned a pale cerulean color.

With a gasp, Lydia opened her eyes. "That's the best I can do."

Professor Hendricks didn't reply right away. She stared at the water in the vase, brows drawn together slightly. At last she said, "It is a very light blue…but it *is* blue. Well done, Lydia."

Instead of looking happy at the praise—and the clear evidence that she'd passed this particular task—Lydia only gave the professor a quick, frightened nod, and then hurried back to her desk, as though worried if she lingered, Professor Hendricks might call out to her that she'd changed her mind and that the water wasn't blue enough after all.

Afterward, the professor started going through the students one by one. Celeste, to my relief, was able to successfully turn a ball of yarn into a small pink afghan, and Helen surprised everyone—and herself—by making an entire chair disappear.

And then Mona was called to the front of the class.

"Miss McGee," Professor Hendricks said. "If you could—make a constellation appear on the ceiling."

Mona didn't even blink. She cupped her hands together and murmured a few words over them, and then opened them just enough to allow a beam of light to emerge—a beam of light that resolved itself into a pattern of glowing stars scattered across the plaster ceiling overhead.

All around me, girls gasped. It was a very beautiful illusion…and also a guarantee that she would move on to the second year, even with her utter failure during the Working With Familiars final.

She closed her hands, and the light disappeared.

"Excellent, Miss McGee," said Professor Hendricks. "You may sit down now."

Grinning, Mona resumed her seat. Philippa leaned over and whispered something to her, and they both giggled.

Usually, the professor would have called a student out for causing that sort of disruption in class. This time, however, she ignored Mona and said, "Juno Hightower."

My heart clenched for my friend. Juno had done her best to act nonchalant about the possibility of being banished to Mundania forever, but I knew how nervous she truly was about passing this class. I found myself praying that Professor Hendricks wouldn't give her anything too difficult to do.

"Miss Hightower," the professor went on. "If you would—turn this dove into a peacock."

And a dove fluttered out of nowhere and landed on the floor in front of Juno.

Her eyes widened with shock. "Um, Professor Hendricks?"

"Yes, Miss Hightower?"

"We haven't done many transmogrifications

this year. Do you really want me to change it completely, or just make it look as if I have?"

Professor Hendricks gazed back at her, expression bland. "Do whatever you think is best, Miss Hightower."

I watched the two of them, lower lip caught in my teeth. Juno was only telling the truth—we had done a lot of work with illusions, as those were much simpler magic. It seemed impossible to believe that the professor expected her to actually change a dove into a peacock. Had she only phrased the question that way because she wanted to see how Juno would react?

If that was the case, it felt like a very dirty trick to me.

Juno was silent for a moment, regarding the dove. At least it seemed like a very well-behaved bird, one that remained where it had first appeared and didn't seem inclined to go flapping about the classroom. For a second, Juno touched her left shoulder with the fingertips of her right hand, as if she expected Fred to be there to lend her moral support. But Fred was back in our room with Flotsam and Jetsam; she'd have to go this one alone.

At last, Juno pressed her thumbs together and made a fanning gesture with both hands, fingers spreading out as if to imitate the extravagant tail feathers of a peacock. Her lips moved as she recited the words of some spell; from where I sat, I couldn't tell for sure whether she was attempting an illusion enchantment, or whether she'd decided that the professor really did mean for her to transmogrify the dove. There was a blink, and the dove disappeared, to be replaced by the very type of bird Professor Hendricks had designated.

True, it was a white peacock whose tail feathers shimmered with opalescent hues rather than the jewel tones of the breed most of us were more familiar with, but still, it looked like a very successful transformation to me.

A murmur of astonishment swept around the room, and for just a moment, the professor's brow lifted, as if she wasn't quite sure of what she was seeing. But then she said, her voice cool, "Very good, Miss Hightower. You may sit down now."

Juno ducked her head, curls bouncing, and headed back to her seat. Her eyes had narrowed as the professor spoke, but it seemed to me she'd decided it was best to remain silent.

As she sat down, the peacock disappeared. I suppose it made sense not to have an enormous bird like that strutting around the classroom, but the way it vanished did seem rather anticlimactic.

Several more of my classmates were put through their paces—not with results as spectacular as Juno's, but they acquitted themselves well enough that I guessed they weren't in any danger of being banished—and then Professor Hendricks called my name.

"Calendula Dobkins."

I did my best not to wince. Yes, my family had a tradition of giving its daughters botanical names, but really, my parents couldn't have come up with something a little less cringe-worthy than "Calendula"?

Despite my discomfort at hearing my full name, I got to my feet and walked to the front of the classroom. Juno shot me an encouraging smile, and Helen and Celeste also did their best to look cheerful. Of course, the three of them had plenty of reasons to appear happy—they'd all done very well with their finals.

Now it was up to me to ensure our little quartet would stay intact.

I took my place in front of the class and did my best not to fidget with the hem of my skirt. Professor Hendricks walked over to me, her buttoned boots creaking faintly with each step. Then she stopped a pace away and extended a hand, palm upward.

On her palm sat a large red apple.

I doubted she was offering me a snack, and so I maintained my silence, waiting for her to speak.

"You see this apple, Miss Dobkins?"

"Yes, Professor Hendricks," I said, hoping all the while that she'd merely want me to make it disappear, or perhaps change its color from red to green.

"Very good. You will turn this apple to gold—not the appearance of gold, mind you, but the element itself. Do you understand?"

I swallowed. What she was asking seemed impossible. Yes, technically it was possible to transmute one material into another—I'd seen demonstrations where skilled magic-workers had been able to turn a lump of coal into a diamond—but it was generally not the sort of thing that was expected of first-year students…especially first-year students whose magic wasn't anywhere close to stable.

Why would she do this to me? Yes, I'd had a few minor successes, but certainly nothing that would indicate I was ready to take on such a high-level piece of magic.

Juno and Helen and Celeste were all watching me with wide, worried eyes. Clearly, they didn't expect I would ever be able to accomplish what Professor Hendricks had asked of me.

I didn't expect to, either.

Anger began to churn in my stomach. Did she want me to fail? Or had she merely detected depths to my magic that I hadn't yet recognized in myself?

I pulled in a breath. I could do this. I *needed* to do this. I wouldn't fail my friends…or myself.

At bottom, all magic flowed from the same source. The only thing we witches and wizards did was provide a focus for it, a way to shape it to our will. Technically, there shouldn't be anything different about turning an apple to gold than making the water in a vase turn blue. It was all about focus.

Unfortunately, my focus seemed to desert me in that moment. I couldn't remember even a simple spell to change the color of my hair, let alone turn an apple into gold.

Don't panic, I admonished myself. *You can do this. Let your magic guide you, rather than you trying to force it.*

Somehow, I managed to make myself think of an apple, how it felt in my hand, what it tasted like. And then I thought of my father's gold pocket watch, how I'd loved to play with it as a little girl, to feel the cool, heavy metal in my palm, to watch the burnished surface catch sunlight from a window or the gleam of a lamp along its edges.

And I looked at the apple in Professor Hendricks' outstretched hand, and I thought of how heavy it would be if it were made of pure gold, how the unexpected weight might make her drop the thing.

The apple's red turned to a warm golden shade, and it rolled out of her hand and hit the floor with a distinct *clank*. Her eyes widened, and she bent to pick it up. One side looked slightly dented from its impact with the wooden surface; pure gold was very soft.

"It's gold," she murmured, and another of those rushes of murmurs made its way around the classroom. Mona McGee was staring at me as if she'd never seen me before. The professor pressed a fingernail against the apple, leaving behind a faint crescent-shaped impression. "Pure gold."

I let out the breath I'd been holding. Surely accomplishing this feat would be enough to ensure my entrance to the second year. I asked, "May I sit down?"

Looking a little dazed, Professor Hendricks replied, "Yes, yes, of course. Thank you, Miss Dobkins."

Trying hard not to look at anyone in particular—mostly so I could keep a grin of triumph from spreading across my mouth—I went back to my desk and sat down. In a daze, I watched several more of my classmates tackle the tasks the professor gave them…none as difficult as my own. In fact, Abigail Andrews botched the simple act of making a bag of marbles disappear and looked as though she was about to burst into tears.

Finally, though, it was all over, and we were released from the classroom. At once, everyone surrounded me, chattering away, asking how I'd managed to accomplish such a feat. Honestly, I didn't have much of an answer to give them, except, "I don't know for sure."

Which was mostly the case. The only think I did know was that I'd had to give my magic free rein to do as it wished, something I'd always avoided in the past.

At length, Juno and Helen and Celeste and I were able to break free and take our lunch outside for an impromptu picnic. The three of them were looking at me in awe, which I hated. Juno, bless her, steered the conversation to light-hearted topics like our upcoming outings with the boys from Master Marco's, and for a while, everything seemed normal enough.

Then Helen said, "It seemed like Professor Hendricks intentionally gave you and Juno much harder tasks than anyone else. Why would she do that?"

Much the same question had been floating around in my mind. Professors at the school were supposed to be impartial, but I couldn't deny that certain biases tended to creep in during the course of the year. Had Professor Hendricks *wanted* us to fail?

No, that was silly.

"Because we kick butt and take names," Juno said proudly, raising her hand for a fist bump. I returned the gesture, since that was obviously what she wanted me to do. At the same time, I had a feeling the true answer was a little more complicated than that.

But we'd all done well, and I wanted to relax and bask in the sunshine and the infinite relief of knowing that, for better or worse, we had all made it through our first year at Miss Primm's.

We would just have to see what happened next.

THE LISTS OF STUDENTS AND THEIR SCORES were posted on the message board outside Miss Primm's office promptly at ten o'clock the next morning. There were three different lists, one for each year, and there was quite a scrum as we all pressed forward to take note of our scores. Anything above six hundred was a passing grade.

We'd already decided to let Juno go forward and look for all our scores, since she was the tallest —and also, as her performance in Physical Activities had shown, not above using her elbows to shove an opponent out of the way. She pressed through the crowd, pushing aside Philippa Carmody, who looked annoyed but apparently thought it better not to say anything.

"Celeste Saint-Michel," Juno called out over her shoulder. "Seven hundred and fifteen. Helen

Jenkins, six hundred and eighty. Juno Hightower, six hundred and ninety-five. And Callie Dobkins—"

I held my breath.

"Eight hundred and five."

Out went the breath I'd been holding. Not just a passing grade, but one that should put me near the top of the class of the incoming second-years. Never in the world would I have thought I'd score so high—but then again, I'd also never thought I'd be able to turn an apple into gold.

My relief and excitement were almost immediately muted, though, as I saw Lydia Vronsky standing off to one side, her eyes red and her nose puffy, as if she'd been crying.

"Are you all right, Lydia?" I asked as Juno shouldered her way back through the crowd to join us.

"No," Lydia replied. Her voice quavered, and she reached up to wipe away the set of new tears that had started to gather in her eyes. "Abigail didn't make it. They came and got her last night."

"'They'?" Juno demanded, having now joined the rest of us. "'They' who?"

Her thin shoulders lifted. "They must have been from DOME. I couldn't see their faces—they were wearing cloaks with the hoods pulled up over their heads."

In a horrible way, I suppose that made some

sense. Better for the people on DOME's banishment teams to remain utterly anonymous so no
one would be able to tell who had come for them
in the night.

Helen's hand went to her mouth, and Celeste
shook her head, expression sad but also resigned.
Anger burned in Juno's dark eyes.

"That's just not right—" she began, but
Celeste cut her off.

"It is how all this works," she said. "We all
knew there was always the risk of not passing, of
being taken away to Mundania. And Abigail did
not do well on her finals."

No, she hadn't. I could perform the cold
mental arithmetic to determine exactly what had
been the final straw, but what would be the point?
Obviously, DOME had known Abigail hadn't
made the grade, and they'd come to take her away
to a world with none of the magic and wonder of
our own.

"I hate it!" Lydia burst out. "I hate that they
can do something like this!"

"I know," I said, even as Helen went over to
the girl and slipped a comforting arm around her
shoulders. "Come on—let's get out of here. We'll
go raid the kitchen and see if they made any more
of those sticky honey buns."

Although Lydia didn't appear as though she
planned to be immediately cheered by this

prospect, she did allow us to draw her away from the corridor outside Miss Primm's office, away from the girls scrambling to see their scores. In a way, the activity seemed rather silly. If they were still here, it meant they had passed. Otherwise, they would have been taken away in the night just as poor Abigail Andrews had.

And though the kitchen did in fact have a new complement of sticky buns for us to steal and take out into the bright August morning, I couldn't quite summon much enthusiasm for eating the treats. I kept thinking of Abigail…kept thinking about the seemingly impossible final task Professor Hendricks had given me.

Several days earlier, I'd said that I would need to keep an eye on Mona McGee. Now it appeared that I would have to do the same with the professor as well….

* * *

Miss Primm's Academy for Wayward Witches continues in Book 2, *Dispelled.*

HEDGEWITCH FOR HIRE

(Mystery/Paranormal romance)

Grave Mistake

Social Medium

Household Demons

Perpetual Potion

Jingle Spells (December 2021)

Wandering Monsters (March 2022)

THE WITCHES OF WHEELER PARK

(Paranormal romance)

Storm Born

Thunder Road

Winds of Change

Mind Games

A Wheeler Park Christmas

Blood Ties

Healing Hands

Wishful Thinking

Smoke and Mirrors (January 2022)

* * *

MISS PRIMM'S ACADEMY FOR WAYWARD
WITCHES*

(Fantasy/Academy Romance)

Misspelled

Dispelled

Expelled

* * *

PROJECT DEMON HUNTERS*

(Paranormal Romance)

Unquiet Souls

Unbound Spirits

Unholy Ground

Unseen Voices

Unmarked Graves

Unbroken Vows

* * *

THE DEVIL YOU KNOW*

(Paranormal Romance)

Sympathy for the Devil

Charmed, I'm Sure

A Wing and a Prayer

* * *

THE WITCHES OF CANYON ROAD*

(Paranormal Romance)

Hidden Gifts

Darker Paths

Mysterious Ways

A Canyon Road Christmas

Demon Born

An Ill Wind

Higher Ground

Haunted Hearts

* * *

THE WITCHES OF CLEOPATRA HILL*

(Paranormal Romance)

Darkangel

Darknight

Darkmoon

Sympathetic Magic

Protector

Spellbound

A Cleopatra Hill Christmas

Impractical Magic

Strange Magic

The Arrangement

Defender

Bad Blood

Deep Magic

Darktide

THE DJINN WARS*

(Paranormal Romance)

Chosen

Taken

Fallen

Broken

Forsaken

Forbidden

Awoken

Illuminated

Stolen

Forgotten

Driven

Unspoken

* * *

THE WATCHERS TRILOGY*

(Paranormal Romance)

Falling Dark

Dead of Night

Rising Dawn

* * *

THE SEDONA FILES*

(Paranormal Romance)

Bad Vibrations

Desert Hearts

Angel Fire

Star Crossed

Falling Angels

Enemy Mine

* * *

TALES OF THE LATTER KINGDOMS*

(Fantasy Romance)

All Fall Down

Dragon Rose

Binding Spell

Ashes of Roses

One Thousand Nights

Threads of Gold

The Wolf of Harrow Hall

Moon Dance

The Song of the Thrush

THE GAIAN CONSORTIUM SERIES*

(Science Fiction Romance)

Beast (free prequel novella)

Blood Will Tell

Breath of Life

The Gaia Gambit

The Mandala Maneuver

The Titan Trap

The Zhore Deception

The Refugee Ruse

* * *

STANDALONE TITLES

Hearts on Fire

Taking Dictation

Golden Heart

Night Music: A Modern Reimagining of The Phantom
of the Opera

Ghost Dance: A Sequel to Gaston Leroux's The
Phantom of the Opera

Flight Before Christmas

* Indicates a completed series

ABOUT THE AUTHOR

USA Today bestselling author Christine Pope has been writing stories ever since she commandeered her family's Smith-Corona typewriter back in grade school. Her work includes paranormal romance, fantasy romance, and science fiction/space opera romance. She makes her home in New Mexico.

Christine Pope on the Web:
www.christinepope.com

 facebook.com/ChristinePopeAuthor

 twitter.com/ChristineJPope

 pinterest.com/ChristineJPope

www.ingramcontent.com/pod-product-compliance
Lightning Source LLC
Chambersburg PA
CBHW052038240626
47153CB00006B/2141